THE KING MAKERS:

THE ADVENTURES OF VINCENT CONNOR

H. BEDFORD-JONES

THE KING MAKERS:

THE ADVENTURES
OF VINCENT CONNOR

H. BEDFORD-JONES

ALTUS PRESS • 2015

EDITED AND DESIGNED BY
Matthew Moring

THANKS TO
Joel Frieman, Everard P. Digges LaTouche and Gerd Pircher

TABLE OF CONTENTS

I

A PRINCE FOR SALE

His companions of the China clubs and legations thought Vincent Connor a wealthy playboy; but his "play" was matching wits in tight places against wily Oriental intriguers.

IN BRISTOW ROAD, Tientsin, were located the head offices of the various Connor enterprises, inherited or acquired by that singular young man, Vincent Connor, rumored to be one of the wealthiest foreign business men in all China. Good will, in that ancient land, counts for a great deal, and various people who had predicted the break-up of the Connor interests after they had passed into the hands of a polo-playing, seemingly idle heir, were at a sad loss to account for the way their prophecies came to naught. But then, very few people were in the confidence of Vincent Connor.

He had just finished the morning mail, and was on the point of departing for the Tientsin Club where he resided nominally, when a special delivery letter arrived. It proved to be from Chang, his father's native partner, who conducted the up-country end of the Connor business from Nanking, the new republican capital. The note, written in flowing Mandarin, was cryptic.

> If you have forty or fifty thousand dollars gold to invest, seek Prince Pho-to at the Pavilion of a Thousand Delights, at Fuchow. The south is far away, except for the merchant who bargains as he goes. It is for you to find one Colonel Moutet of the French embassy, who also travels south.

Connor was tempted to laugh at this, but knew better than to laugh at any message from Chang, who was in most intimate touch with China's affairs. Also, as it happened, he did have ten

*"Here is ten thousand pounds," said
Connor to the incredulous Russian.*

thousand pounds, an intended bribe recently acquired, from
certain unscrupulous gentry, whose point of view regarding the
future of China did not coincide with that of Connor.

"Prince Pho-to—huh!" grunted Connor, skepticism in his
dark-blue eyes, a frown upon his wide-jawed, wide-angled features. Yale had not dimmed his childhood grasp of China's
tongue or customs; and in the two years since taking over the
business, he had gone far in knowledge.

"That's no Chinese name; sounds like Annamese, or else a
joke," he reflected. "And Fuchow! Why the devil go away down
there? Still, old Chang has scented something, sure enough.
Better look up this chap Moutet. He must be around these
parts, if Chang said to find him."

Apparently no easy task, in a city that held the flotsam of
half a dozen nations, from Russian refugees to Italian exiles,
and teemed with business and intrigue. Therefore Connor was
somewhat startled to run slap upon his man at the first cast—
to find him, indeed, a guest at the Tientsin Club, and to see
him sitting at a table across the room as he lunched.

He studied the man, sensing an adversary. Moutet was
forty-odd, gray at the temples, with the hard, precise features
of a martinet, a steel-trap mouth, black eyes merciless as steel.

Evidently a man in rigid self-restraint, therefore an extremist who would not know how to relax in moderation. Half a dozen decorations. Lithe, active, vigorous. Connor made up his mind on the instant; he needed information, first of all, and swiftly weighed different schemes. No, he must use the bungalow—his disguise would not do for a long trip. Besides, he had no need of it in the south, where he was unknown.

Thus resolved, he took prompt action. Moutet, he discovered, was in charge of a typically French "mission" at Mukden, was now on leave, and was one of the most important French undercover officers in Asia—in other words, a semi-secret agent cloaking his diplomatic work behind scientific and industrial work. Down south in Yünnan, a French colony in fact if not in name, the Connor interests had large timber monopolies, under the name of the Laoyang Company. Upon these facts Connor based his action.

His "bungalow" was in reality a mandarin's pleasure palace, which his father had converted into a residence. Connor rarely used it; Hung, the old family servitor, remained in charge. So, at two that afternoon, Connor called up Hung on the wire from his club rooms.

"A dinner for two, at eight to-night, Hung," he said. "Chinese style, but with cocktails and no rice wine. With the first few courses serve that Vouvray '16, and plenty of it. With the later courses, the Chateau Spire '97, in the large goblets. Afterward, the Napoleon cognac. And plenty of that, also."

IT WAS no difficult matter to reach Colonel Moutet by telephone, and once he had his man, Connor spoke in his none too good French, using the high, sing-song tones that went with his assumed character.

"This is M. Wang Erh Yu of the Laoyang Company—the timber interests in Yünnan," Connor said. "I am the vice president and general manager, and there are several matters of policy which I should like to discuss with you. If M. le Colonel will honor me with his company at dinner, at my residence here—"

Colonel Moutet was not averse to dining with a wealthy Chinese, and Connor arranged to call for him later.

His nostrils widened and lips thickened by cotton pads, his black hair coarsened with grease, his sunburned features and hands yellowed by a saffron infusion, his European garments cunningly tailored to give an air of awkwardness, "Mr. Wang" carried off his dinner guest promptly on time, to a dinner such as Moutet had seldom eaten, with wines which the appreciative Frenchman found miraculous. Mr. Wang himself ate very little.

There was enough talk of business to appease any possible suspicion—tentative agreements made, plans discussed. Moutet proved to be sympathetic, sternly bound by orders, with a clear understanding of native problems and customs; he had a fa-natical regard for duty, though when Mr. Wang mentioned the recent revolt in Annam, Moutet did not hesitate to express his contempt for bureaucracy. The old brown cognac loosened his tongue a bit, perhaps.

"Between ourselves, of course," said the colonel, "the whole affair was incredibly bungled. Whole villages were destroyed and needless air bombardments were carried out. The penal commission was illegal. The executions and sentences were barbarous. That is no way to make the Annamese love us! They are burdened with intolerable taxes. Some day, mark me, there'll be an explosion in Annam."

"Because of stupid oppression?"

"Yes." Moutet shrugged. "Plenty of us see the mistakes; what can we do except carry out orders? I myself leave to-morrow on a most unpleasant, even degrading errand—yet I must do my best. Look at the opium monopoly, despite the decrees of the Chamber in Paris!"

"Did you ever," queried Mr. Wang carelessly, "hear of an Annamese mandarin or ruler by the name of Pho-to? I've heard the name; I cannot recall in what connection."

"Hm!" Colonel Moutet started, but instantly became casual again. "Yes, a good deal was heard of him down there. The heir to the throne, or so called, and a man greatly loved and revered by natives. A dangerous man, from our viewpoint. I understand he has brains and has made foreign contacts. He was involved in the revolt, but fled into Chinese territory somewhere. No one knows just where he is, I believe."

Mr. Wang blinked behind his thick spectacles. "Indeed! Let us hope that French rule will save Annam and Yünnan from the chaos which has enveloped China!"

Later, Mr. Wang took his guest back to the club—and thirty minutes later was packing his own bag, preparatory to catching the boat leaving for Shanghai in the morning.

"Evidently," he reflected, "this excellent colonel is going to see Prince Pho-to, and will perform his errand to the letter, even if it revolts him. It must be disagreeable indeed! Probably it is even illegal; so much the better."

He did not forget to pack the ten thousand pounds in crisp black-and-white Bank of England notes.

ON THE way to Shanghai, Connor saw little of Moutet; there were other French officers aboard and all flocked together, after the manner of their caste.

It was different after changing to a Merchants' Line boat for Fuchow. Their mess seats were together, and acquaintance began with the first meal; Connor's name was unknown to the Frenchman, since the various Connor enterprises went by Chinese names, and Moutet was far from recognizing Mr. Wang in this scrupulously dressed young American.

It was late afternoon when they entered the Min River and bore up for Pagoda Anchorage, for the transfer to steam launches. Here Moutet departed in the French consular launch, and Connor went on to the city, nine miles above, by the regular craft, landing at the Hwang-sung wharf and taking a hotel sedan chair up to the Brand House. After a wash-up, he sallied forth to the office of the local Connor agent, a sleek little man of great efficiency, who welcomed the head of the firm with much éclat, though it was just closing time.

"This wholly unworthy person needs your help, great maternal uncle," said Connor in the old stilted phrases of Mandarin.

"All that this humble slave owns is at the disposal of the venerable ancestor!"

"Tell me what you know about the Pavilion of a Thousand Delights. And its occupants."

"It is a viceroy's palace in the higher ground beyond the Nangtai district," said the local manager. "Long vacant, it was occupied several months ago by a foreigner—"

"Prince Pho-to of Annam," said Connor. "Go on."

The sleek eyes blinked. "Exactly. With him are Annamese servants and twenty wives; but there is talk that his creditors are many and he has been selling jewels. Also, the French have spies watching him, although his own servants are faithful. I think he will be sold out by one of the two men with him."

"Eh?" Connor frowned at this, which sounded involved. "Which two men?"

"The white men. One is French, an army deserter. The other is an old Russian, a cripple."

"Which one would sell him out?"

"I do not know. It is only gossip."

"Very well. Now I have important work for you. I wish an interview with this French courtier at my hotel, within the hour if possible; I wish an interview with the Russian at the Pavilion of a Thousand Delights at a later hour this evening. Provide a palanquin for me with bearers who may be trusted implicitly."

"This slave will obey the orders of the great maternal ancestor."

"One thing more. This Prince Pho-to himself—does he speak English or Mandarin?"

"No. He speaks only his own barbarian tongue, and French."

"Good enough."

Connor departed. He had given his agent an almost impossible commission, yet he knew it would be fulfilled.

H E WA S right. Before he finished dinner, a chit arrived from his agent:

> The first will come soon after this. An interview with the second at nine o'clock. A chair will await you at the door.

With a satisfied nod, Connor finished his dinner, left instructions at the desk regarding a visitor, and went to his room. He had no more than got his pipe well drawing, when a knock came at his door; a short man with wide shoulders and bronzed features, a vigorous and direct manner, tailored whites, entered and bowed.

"M'sieu' Connor? Allow me."

From the pasteboard extended, Connor found that he was dealing with one M. Raymond Delille, formerly *avocat* at the Court of Appeals, Toulouse. In a flash he had a glimmer of the man's past; a lawyer, perhaps involved in some disgrace, enlisting in the Colonial forces, later on deserting, to guide the destinies of this rebelling prince and share his fortune, literally enough. Connor smiled, waved his visitor to a chair and a drink.

"Do you speak English, M. Delille—no? Then pray pardon my hesitant French. As you may be aware, it is the habit of Americans to come bluntly to the point, so let us do it. I believe you are acquainted with Colonel Moutet?"

The eyes of Delille hardened, though not before a flicker of apprehension darted in them.

"I know of him at least, *m'sieu',*" he replied cautiously.

"You know that he is here in Fuchow?"

"No! Impossible!" The startled surprise was genuine beyond any question. Connor smiled and took a cigarette from his jade-and-gold case.

"Come, M. Delille; we are not children, you and I. You occupy a certain position with the prince, eh? Never mind what position I occupy; I asked you to come here in order to tell you about Moutet, and to ask you a certain question."

From his pocket, Connor took the sheaf of Bank of England notes and carelessly riffled them in his fingers. They fascinated the widening gaze of the Frenchman.

"Understand me," went on Connor easily. "I am in no way acting contrary to Colonel Moutet or his desires. He is in absolute ignorance of my business, as I am of his; but I suspect that he will make you certain propositions. Well and good. Here in my hand is fifty thousand dollars, gold, in cash. In the event that Moutet made you an offer, and you had this money to cast into the scales with it—would you accept?"

Delille looked up, his eyes dilating.

"An offer—"

"To betray Prince Pho-to, if we put it bluntly."

Delille grimaced. "*Diantre!* Blunt you certainly are. Well, *m'sieu'*, I am not a fool. Do I understand that you offer me this money, here and now?"

Connor laughed. "By no means. Moutet will probably communicate with you to-night or in the morning. Do not mention me to him. If, as I believe, his plans are in entire agreement with my own, I shall turn over the money to you—half in advance, half upon consummation of the work. This, I believe, is satisfactory?"

The other nodded, and drew a deep breath.

"Fifty thousand cash! It is eminently satisfactory, my dear American! I'll communicate with you after Moutet sees me, eh? Good."

"But no mention of me, mind!" warned Connor, and the other promised volubly.

"Dirty rat!" muttered Connor as his visitor departed.

On the evidence he had acquired, he no longer doubted that the mission which Moutet had mentioned was to get rid somehow of the menace presented by Prince Pho-to; by abducting him and getting him back to French territory, perhaps by killing him. Connor had heard much about the man on his way south, about his integrity, his popularity, his hatred of the despotic French rule which gripped the empire of his fathers.

And Pho-to, so far as Connor could discover, was next to helpless. None of the great powers had interests in Annam, none of them had any reason to help the prince or to protect him. In seizing or killing him, France could violate Chinese soil with impunity, for all China was in anarchy. Connor had begun to feel an acute sympathy for this fugitive.

To such affairs as this, rather than to piling up more wealth in business, Vincent Connor had devoted himself. To this indefinable cause of justice, of aiding the oppressed, he flung his weight of wealth and connections, his personal abilities, his knowledge of China and its people. Not the least of his aids was his own reputation; the last person to be suspected of such things was the coxcomb and dandy, the young spendthrift from college who had inherited the Connor fortunes.

AT NINE-FIFTEEN Connor left the hotel, clad in faultless evening clothes which did not betray the little automatic nestling under his armpit. As he came down the steps, a sedan chair was brought forward; he stepped in silently, and the chair sped away, two men trotting before and after the bearers, with torches.

He had a brief and unforgettable vision of Fuchow by night—the far-flung Chinese city across the river glimmering and shimmering with lights, the two bridges sketched against the darkness by their lanterns, the electric lights of the Nangtai section stretching up the hillsides; then he was in darkness, out of the streets, the bearers padding along a hill road.

Of the Pavilion of a Thousand Delights, he could make out little. Gates in a wall were thrown open, they passed through gardens, and came finally to a lighted doorway where waited a brown Annamese servant. Connor stepped out of his chair, a door was opened, and he found himself in a room whose floor was thick with rugs, whose walls were high with bookshelves, in a soft glow of light from half a dozen Chinese lamps.

Waiting for him was the crippled Russian.

Connor found himself returning the bow of a man whose hair was white, whose face was seamed by age and sufferings, whose body was twisted awkwardly as though wrenched askew by giant hands, yet whose evening attire was faultless as his own. The face of the man was remarkable; it was like wood wrought by the adze, so harsh were its angles, and the thin, bloodless lips made an imperceptible line beneath the clipped mustache, but the eyes were piercing, brilliant blue as though lighted by eternal youth.

"I believe you are Mr. Connor?" said the Russian in fluent English. "I am Ivan Serovitch, Comrade Ivan if you like, formerly a prince of the Litovsk House."

The savage irony of the man showed in his acid voice. Connor smiled.

"Prince Ivan, should I say?" he returned, with the warm affability which made men like and trust him. "I do not care particularly for the titles of Soviet democracy, myself."

"Will you be seated?" Serovitch indicted a chair by the table, where a tray of liqueurs was in evidence. "I am ignorant of the nature of your business."

"Oh, it is extremely commercial business, I assure you," said Connor. From his pocket he produced the sheaf of bank notes and laid them on the table, and across them faced the keen blue eyes of his host. "There is ten thousand pounds in cash. Will you count it?"

"In cash? Are you mad—or is this some jest?" The Russian seized the sheaf of notes and glanced through them. He replaced them and frowned at his visitor. "Well?"

"They can be yours, if you will. Every one knows your master is practically done for; his money and credit are exhausted, he is friendless; the net is closing upon him. Well, finish it and earn this packet of notes."

A mortal pallor swept into the distorted face of the Russian.

He gripped the table edge with both hands, staring at Connor from blazing eyes.

"You mean it?" he whispered.

"There is the money. What better proof?"

Serovitch passed a hand across his brow, relaxed.

"Let me tell you something, Mr. Connor," he said after a moment. "For ten years I have been the tutor and friend of Prince Pho-to; his destiny has been in my hands, his character has upgrown under my eyes. I have gained a deep admiration for his integrity, for his high and noble spirit. Adversity has not shaken nor altered him. He is truly what Confucius was wont to call the superior man."

Connor shrugged with affected cynicism.

"You may write his epitaph, then," he observed. "Come! Your decision?"

The blue eyes flamed at him.

"Mr. Connor, in my younger days I would have answered your insult with a dagger in your vile heart," said the Russian hoarsely. "As it is, I can only tell you to take your filthy money and get out of here before I call the servants to whip you out. Go!"

A LAUGH broke from Connor. He leaned forward, his eyes very warm, and put out his hand.

"You are a rare man, Ivan Serovitch. Give me your hand! I am proud to know you. I came here, a stranger to you and to Delille, and I had to test you both. I knew one of you was a traitor, perhaps both. The hand of France is already closing upon you, and I myself am running too great risks to take any chances. Now let us start afresh. Your hand!"

The Russian stared in slow comprehension.

"So!" he returned. "You—you don't know how close you were to death!"

Their hands met. Then Connor pushed the money across the table.

"Take it, for your master. It cost me nothing; it is a political bribe I snatched from both the givers and the taker. Now it will serve a real purpose."

"Is this another trick?" Serovitch glared, incredulous and suspicious. "Why are you here? For whom are you acting?"

"For myself," said Connor, and briefly sketched his own position. "You see, these things amuse me. Occasionally reward comes, when one meets a man like you, or like Colonel Moutet."

Serovitch started. "Moutet! That devil—you know him?"

"I arrived in Fuchow to-day, with him," said Connor quietly. "He is not a devil, but a man who obeys orders at all costs, right or wrong. He is here upon a mission which revolts his every instinct, yet he will perform it. You can guess what it is. And Delille—"

"Delille!" breathed the Russian. "The deserter, the renegade, bound to us by every tie of gratitude—"

"Plays the part of Judas," said Connor. "Listen, my friend! Don't let that man suspect that you know. Leave him to me; rather, we shall meet the treachery together. I'll have more details to-morrow."

The chin of Serovitch sank on his breast.

"I have feared this," he said gloomily. "Assassination, perhaps. They will stop at nothing. In two days I will have an answer from the British. If we can reach Singapore and stay there, he is safe. Gracious God, how I have worked for it! Undoubtedly the French know this, know that the British will give us protection there. This is why Moutet is here, you see? He means to stop us."

"And you really had no money?"

"Not a piastre," said Serovitch. "No credit. The prince has magnificent jewels, but we could not sell them here. This money of yours—"

"Not mine," and Connor smiled. "Yours."

The Russian looked at him for a moment, then came to his feet.

"Come. I want you to meet the prince. I will tell him all these things."

Serovitch led the way to a curtain, pushed it aside, opened a door after knocking, and ushered Connor into a room where a man sat at a desk writing. The man looked up. He was a typical Annamese, small, thin-featured, in European garments. The Russian clicked his heels and saluted.

"M. le Prince," he said in French, "I beg leave to present a friend, M. Connor, an American. He has come to warn me of danger and to lend certain help."

Prince Pho-to shook hands with Connor, spoke a few words in French, then echoed the word "danger" inquiringly. The Russian shrugged.

"He informs me that Colonel Moutet arrived in Fuchow to-day."

The Annamese made a quiet gesture.

"Very well, my friend," he said to Serovitch. "I understand. It is finished; I shall fight no more, but accept my fate. We have no money, no friends, no hope."

Serovitch laid the packet of notes on the desk.

"On the contrary, M. le Prince, here is ten thousand English pounds, and with it the assurance of help. Moutet's presence means that they are desperate, that a refuge will be given us at Singapore. Thanks to M. Connor."

The thin features lifted; the strained, earnest eyes looked into those of Connor for a moment, then the thin brown hand came out and caught at that of Connor.

"Why you should do this for us I do not know or ask. My friend, I cannot express my thanks."

"Confucius said," returned Connor smilingly, "that it is insulting for the superior man to express thanks to a friend. There is a deep meaning in the words, your highness."

The prince smiled.

TOWARD NOON of the following day, Delille came

again to the Brand House and was brought directly to Connor's room. He was excited, eager, tense.

"I have seen Moutet," he said in a low voice, his eyes very bright. "He offers me full pardon for all offenses and a post in the Bureau des Indigenes."

Connor's brows lifted. "For what?"

Delille came closer, glanced around, breathed soft words.

"To-night I will send away most of the servants. At nine, Moutet arrives for a meeting with that damned Russian, Serovitch; three other officers come with him, the car waits. With my help, four can do the work. The Russian will be eliminated, the prince will be carried off!"

"And if he resists?" queried Connor. The Frenchman laughed and shrugged.

"So much the worse for him. It does not matter, really. And—the money?"

"To-night," said Connor. "I shall be at the Pavilion myself, and lend a hand."

"Good! So much the better. Ask for me when you come, you comprehend?"

Delille departed in high spirits.

Connor set forth after the siesta hour for the office of his agent. As he was passing the local branch of the Yokohama Specie Bank, he came face to face with Prince Ivan Serovitch, who was just emerging. The face of the Russian lighted up.

"Ah, my friend! I have received news from Singapore—it is arranged! We depart by the boat to-morrow."

"Moutet strikes to-night," said Connor. The other started.

"What? You are certain?"

"Delille expects him at nine."

A grimace passed across the pallid, hard-angled features. "Very well."

"Will you receive suggestions?" asked Connor gently.

"With all my heart!"

"You will be asked to meet Moutet. Agree. Agree to everything. Be ill. Leave all arrangements in the hands of Delille,
you comprehend? Moutet arrives at nine; he will be precise. I
will arrive ten minutes before the hour, or will send a friend in
my name."

"Eh? But we should post guards—" Connor tapped him on
the arm. "Your place is watched. Why attempt to spoil their
effort and make them take some other plan? Better to finish
the thing and remove future danger."

"You are right," said the Russian slowly. "But the prince—"

Connor chuckled, then spoke rapidly. "Can you do it?" he
concluded. The crippled old Russian broke into a laugh, clapped
him on the shoulder, then departed, walking with queer, twisted
steps.

Going on to the office of his agent, Connor presently secured
what he wanted, and then departed for a sightseeing tour of
the river and its teeming life. He was not surprised to see that
two French river gunboats were riding at anchor off the foreign
concession.

AFTER DINING in leisurely fashion, Connor mounted
to his own room and there sat down to adopt the spectacles,
yellowish tint, and altered features of Mr. Wang—even, with a
drop or two of collodion, contriving to give his eyelids an
oblique angle. He did not have Mr. Wang's wardrobe at hand,
but his agent had supplied white pongee garments which served
the purpose very well. At eight thirty Connor surveyed himself
in the glass, and was satisfied. Five minutes later he entered the
sedan chair which awaited him, and was on his way.

At ten minutes before nine, his sedan chair halted at the
same doorway as on the previous night. The Annamese on guard
there barred his way, but at the name of Connor, ushered him
into the book-walled room. It was empty. Finding himself alone,
Connor lighted a cigarette and sank into a chair, only to stiffen
and turn his head, listening.

From this room opened two inner doors: one to the room

of the prince, the other to the left. From this second door, Connor caught strange sounds; a pounding of feet, the murmur of hoarse voices, and then a sudden cry. He started erect, and the door flew open to show the twisted figure of Serovitch. In the Russian's hand was a saber that dripped with fresh blood.

"What has happened?" exclaimed Connor, forgetting his role. "What has gone wrong?"

Serovitch stepped forward, staring incredulously.

"You!" he exclaimed. "But—but this is marvelous! Except for the voice, I would not have guessed—"

"Ah! I forgot to introduce myself," said Connor. "I am Mr. Wang."

"Come." Serovitch stood aside at the open door, and gestured. Connor stepped forward.

The next room was a large, nearly empty salon. Lying beside a heavy chair was the body of Delille, still clasping a saber in his hand, a great gash in his throat. Serovitch laughed.

"Judas is repaid," he said in a voice of steel. Connor shrugged.

"Just as well, I suppose," he observed. "But there's no time to waste. All is arranged?"

"Everything. Bring Moutet in here."

"With Delille there on the floor? He'd give the alarm instantly."

The Russian stooped, picked up a tattered rug, and flung it out over the dead figure.

"What better?"

"Right. Does your servant speak Chinese?"

"No; but he speaks French fluently. This devil sent off all but the two men."

"No matter. I'll get back in there to receive them. All hangs on that."

Connor returned to the reception room. He was counting heavily on the moment of mental confusion when Moutet recognized Mr. Wang; it would fog that keen brain, cover up the trap which otherwise Moutet might suspect. As he had said, all hinged upon that.

THE ENTRANCE door opened, held by the Annamese servant. Into the room stepped Colonel Moutet, three other men behind him—young, eager men, all four of them in mufti, eyes gleaming. To these others, here was adventure, romance, peril, and to them it mattered nothing if the destiny of other men hung upon their action.

Moutet halted dead at sight of his host.

"M. Wang! You here?" he ejaculated in surprise. Mr. Wang bowed and smiled.

"I am delighted to see you again, M. le Colonel! My friend M. Delille is indisposed, and asked me to meet you. He desires to have a word with you. Meantime, his highness the prince would be pleased to receive your friends, while they await us. I will announce them."

He went to the door of the prince's study, knocked, and opened it to see the figure at the desk. Over his shoulder, a glance showed him Moutet, tensed at this opportunity, speaking rapidly to his three companions. Connor stepped back.

"*Messieurs,* his highness will receive you. There is no ceremony; pray enter, M. le Colonel, will you have the goodness to step this way?"

The three officers observed nothing; Moutet was too much astonished to notice at once the lack of plausibility in this reception. He turned to the door of the other room with Mr. Wang, who opened it and closed it again after him.

Standing half hidden by the curtain, Mr. Wang waited a moment. There came a choked voice from the study, a scraping of feet; the three officers reappeared, hastily crossing the room, half carrying, half thrusting, a slender Annamese figure. The entrance door swung open and closed again. They were gone with their prey.

Mr. Wang opened the door at his hand, and passed into the salon.

Colonel Moutet stood there, a man thunderstruck. At one side had appeared Serovitch, silent, sardonic; coming forward toward the Frenchman was Prince Pho-to, smiling slightly. Mr. Wang locked the door, and at the sound Moutet glanced around, perceived everything.

"This is an unexpected pleasure, M. le Colonel," said the grave-eyed Annamese, and Moutet bowed to mask his emotion. "You have come, perhaps, to invite me back to my own country?"

Moutet bit his lip. "I have certain offers to lay before your highness," he said stiffly.

"Perhaps," said Mr. Wang, "you would care to see the late M. Delille?"

With his foot he stirred back the rug, enough to show the dead face of the traitor. At this, Moutet perceived that he was lost. In the uncertain light of the lanterns, his face was white, tense.

"Come!" said the prince quietly. "We know everything, *monsieur.*"

Mr. Wang intervened. "Perhaps not everything, your highness." He turned and met the gaze of the Frenchman. "Well, *m'sieu'?* Just how far do your instructions go? You have violated the neutrality of China. Your men have carried off a man whom they too hastily assumed to be the prince. The offense is a grave one. You alone knew the prince by sight, and of course—"

"Trickster!" said Moutet in a stifled voice. "Who are you?"

"I am China," said Mr. Wang calmly, looking Moutet in the eyes. "You must pay for this offense, *monsieur.* You will leave here in a few moments, and for three weeks you will travel upcountry, with very good companions who will see to your comfort and safety."

"You seem very certain that you have beaten me," said Moutet, and his face was like death.

"Careful, *monsieur!*" warned Mr. Wang. "I think I know what is in your mind. You are a gentleman; yet you have your orders. I warn you that what I do not know, I suspect. You hoped to remove Prince Pho-to, if not by one means, then by another. Respect my warning, for I have guarded against everything—

"Except this!" said Moutet.

And with the word, he whipped out a tiny pistol from his sleeve, firing point-blank at the prince—only to fall sidewise in the very act, as Mr. Wang stooped and jerked the rug from under his feet. Smiling, Mr. Wang looked down at the fallen man.

"You should not telegraph your blows, as they say in America, M. le Colonel."

The prince had disappeared from the room. Moutet looked up at the smiling Mr. Wang, at the acid-eyed Russian; then, with a swift gesture, he seized the fallen pistol and held it to his ear as he pressed the trigger. This time, he did not miss.

S O M E   W E E K S after this event, in his rooms at the Tien-tsin Club, Connor was enjoying a pre-dinner drink with a friend from the British legation.

The Briton picked up a magnificent paper-weight from the table, a bit of wondrous old brown Han jade that dated back two thousand years, fashioned into the semblance of a fu-lion. He examined it with appreciation.

"I say, old chap—a marvelous bit of *han yu*, what? Did you pick it up here?"

"A present to me," said Connor, adjusting his dress tie before the mirror. "From a friend of mine named Pho-to."

"Eh, what?" The other glanced suspiciously at him. "Pho-to, eh? I suppose that's some sort of an American joke, what? Photograph and all that. Quite so! You're never serious, are you?"

"No, I'm too busy—playing jokes," and Connor chuckled.

I I

HOUSE OF MISSING MEN

*Vincent Connor wondered why a Russian
countess should invite his friend to dinner
in the French concession at Tientsin; and
the answer was sudden and grim.*

CONNOR WAS dressing for dinner, in his rooms at the Tientsin Club, when Vanessen barged in for a drink. Young Vanessen was a "griffin"—China coast equivalent of tenderfoot—in charge of the accounting for the Harris people; and Connor liked his frank boyishness and his Yale anecdotes. To-night, however, he observed that Vanessen, for all his exuberance of spirit, was a trifle uneasy beneath the surface.

"No wonder you're worried," he observed critically. "That dress tie of yours is a positive atrocity, Van, and those lapels are quite too wide. And do I smell *Fleur de Nuit?*"

Vanessen regarded the perfectly tailored figure of his host a bit wistfully.

"All very well for you, Connor," he said with good humor. "You inherited a mint of money, business interests extending over half China, and more or less good looks. All you have to do is sign checks, play polo, race your ponies, and let your tailor tell you the latest in London styles. Pretty soft, boy, pretty soft! Never mind my lapels. You wouldn't think about them if you knew where I was dining to-night."

"Yeah?" Connor lit a cigarette, glanced into the mirror and adjusted his waistcoat. "Bet your *comprador* is taking you to a Chinese dinner."

"Nix on that stuff!" Vanessen waved his hand with mock disdain. "She's a princess and a nifty blonde—get me? A real princess, too. Russian."

"Most of 'em are real," said Connor, unexcitedly. "Princesses in Russia are common as fleas in Spain, Van. Lot of Russian nobility in these parts; like fleas, too, they live off other people."

Vanessen flushed slightly.

"See here, Connor, I don't like the implication," he said. "Princess Orloff isn't any adventuress. Her crowd are not all angels, of course, but she's all right. Why, she's even in a bit of diplomatic work!"

Connor's fingers seemed to freeze against his tie-ends.

"Yes?" he said. "What sort? For what government?"

"Well, I'm not positive; she didn't say exactly. There were a couple of diplomats at her house last night, though—an Italian attaché and a British chap. She's on the level, Connor."

"Undoubtedly. Didn't mean to insinuate she wasn't, old chap," and Connor turned with a smile to pick up his drink and sip it. "Where does she live?"

"French concession, just off the Avenue Kléber. If you'd like to go around with me—"

"Sorry, I'm tied up to-night. Another time, by all means. By the way, Van, is anything bothering you? Must say you look a bit nervous."

"Bit of an eye strain from too much work, perhaps." Vanessen rose. "Well, thanks for the drink and the advice, old man. If I make a ten-strike one of these days I'll drop around and investigate your tailor; I must say his handiwork has always intrigued me. Night!"

Alone, Connor lit a cigarette and sipped at his drink reflectively. His wide-angled features with their odd blue eyes and black hair were half frowning; he liked young Vanessen, and was afraid the chap might be drifting in with the wrong crowd, although he had never heard of any Princess Orloff.

This was not surprising, for Vincent Connor would of course know no one not in his own pleasure-loving set. As Vanessen had just said, he was rather an idler, with vast business connections inherited from his father, a faultless tailor, and no ambition

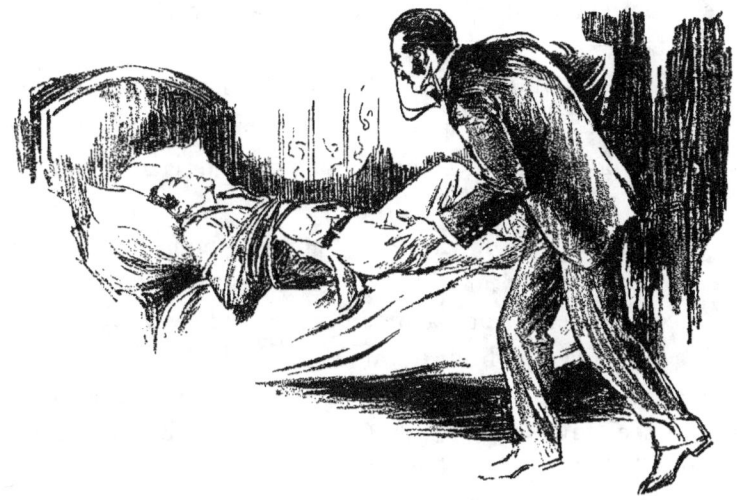

Forsythe discovered a man, well trussed, unconscious.

in life except to dress perfectly, pass his time in vapid amusement or rapid sports, and avoid matrimonial entanglements. Such, at least, was the general idea of Vincent Connor as others saw him.

The few who really knew him, however—the few who knew to what ends he devoted his amazing knowledge of China, its language, its customs, its people—knew otherwise.

Turning to the telephone, Connor obtained his number and presently had his general manager on the wire.

"Mr. Connor speaking," he said, then lapsed into Mandarin, which he had spoken from boyhood. "Do you know anything about a Princess Orloff who has a place off the Avenue Kléber in the French concession?"

"I have heard the name, but know nothing of the person," came the reply.

"Then get me a report on her first thing in the morning, please," said Connor, and so dismissed the entire matter from his mind for that night.

He was breakfasting the next morning when Winslow, of

the *Times,* entered the dining room of the club and came over to his table.

"Morning, Connor. May I join you? Thanks. Beastly wet morning, eh? I've been out on a rotten story, too."

"That's no novelty in Tientsin," said Connor lazily. "Lady in the case?"

"Nope. Chap got in with some gambling house, apparently, went the works, shot himself. Rather decent young griffin, by all accounts. Left a note saying he'd gambled away everything he had—made a night of it, came back to his hotel, probably sent off a letter to his people, then plugged himself. Blast it all, I can't see why a chap wants to blow out his brains merely because he's flung his roll into the gutter!"

"Evidence of no brains to begin with," commented Connor. "Who was the chap? British?"

"No, American. Some dashed queer name—oh, yes! Vanessen."

APPARENTLY, CONNOR was the only person to guess that Vanessen's suicide had anything to do with the Princess Orloff. And Connor, though he might guess a good deal, knew nothing.

Not all his sources could discover much about the nifty blonde. She had arrived in Tientsin a month previous, with a French passport, but coming from America; she had leased the villa off the Avenue Kléber for a year and had engaged French servants; she never went to the races, dances, or other diversions of the European colony. After two days of ceaseless effort, Connor was unable to find a person who knew her or who could so much as describe her.

On the third day he dropped his investigation.

"Vanessen was trapped," he told himself reflectively. "For some reason they wanted to use him—whoever 'they' may be! He was decoyed, fleeced, probably gave heavy I O U's; their idea was to get him in their power. Instead, he killed himself. Hm! They'd probably know me only too well—"

He summoned his general manager and instructed him to look after the Connor interests for the next fortnight or more.

"I'm catching the Hinyo Marti to-night for a month in Japan," he said. "See that the matter is not kept secret. Let everybody know it, in fact. Meantime, get me a berth on the night train for Peking."

At Peking, a deserted city of the dead under its new name of Peiping, Connor remained in seclusion for three days with his Chinese branch agent there. Those three days effected a tremendous change in Vincent Connor.

The fourth morning saw him dressed in none too trim hand-me-downs. A budding black mustache materially altered his features, as did the budding sideburns down past his ears. His healthy sunburned tan had been bleached out to a curious pallor which in itself would have rendered him unrecognizable. To complete his new identity he donned large glasses with black rims and faintly tinted lenses of plain glass, and faced his grinning agent.

"Does this humble slave seem like another person to his august maternal relative?" he asked in Mandarin.

The yellow man bowed.

"My unworthy eyes do not recognize the appearance of my honorable superior," he replied. "May I inquire his distinguished name and titles?"

"I," said Connor with a chuckle, "am John Forsythe, in the employ of the Laoyang Company at Tientsin."

Next morning, indeed, he took over a desk in the head office at Tientsin—the Laoyang Company being that branch of the Connor interests which dealt in timber. As befitted the chief clerk, he had a private office.

At five that afternoon Mr. Forsythe, carrying a cane and walking with a slight limp, came up the steps of the villa off the Avenue Kléber. To the French maid who opened the door he handed his card.

"I want to see the Princess Olga, or somebody," he said, to

find that she knew no English. She hesitated, then admitted him and departed. Presently a sallow man in tweeds, with a distinct English accent, appeared holding his card and announced himself as secretary to the princess.

"The nature of your business, Mr. Forsythe?" he inquired coldly.

"Well, it's like this," said Forsythe. "I want to find out about a friend of mine named Vanessen, and I expect somebody here can tell me—"

"You are mistaken, sir," intervened the other. "There is no person here of that name, certainly."

"I know that," said Forsythe. "Listen, now, I just got here last night, see? I'm chief clerk with a lumber company—been down at Shanghai until now. I came out with Vanessen and we're friends. He wrote me last week about knowing this princess here and so forth, so when I got here and found out about his being dead, I thought maybe you folks could throw some light upon the whole business."

The secretary listened to all this with a somewhat agitated air, then drew out a chair.

"Will you sit down?" he said. "I do not know if the princess—Princess Orloff is the name—is at liberty, but I shall be glad to take her your card. Perhaps she may know more about your friend than I do."

Forsythe nodded, sat down, produced a cheap American cigarette and stared about the quietly handsome room.

"Hooked 'em!" he thought jubilantly. "And I ought to be just the man they want—though why they want some one remains to be seen. That secretary chap is no Englishman; he overdid the part. Looked like a Russian, rather."

A WOMAN swept into the room—blond, svelte, Paris-gowned, touched with barbaric jewels. She was perhaps thirty, but looked younger. When she put out her hand to Forsythe her whole manner was appealing, friendly, luring. Her liquid dark eyes were belied by thin and perhaps cruel lips, but one forgot these in her warm cordiality; her features were piquant, impulsive, charming. Her fluent English was tinged with a slight and delightful accent.

"I am so happy to see you, Mr. Forsythe!" she exclaimed, taking a chair and motioning him to another close by. "Your poor friend spoke more than once of you—it was such a shock to us all! You see, we liked him very much indeed."

"He was a fine fellow," said Forsythe. "Are you the princess he wrote about?"

"But of course!" She laughed quickly. "Princess Orloff—but Olga to my friends. Have you been long in Tientsin?"

"Only a day. I came around here to see if I could find—"

She lifted her hand; swift pain clouded her brilliant eyes.

"Ah, of course! My friend, I can tell you little about him. I think he fell in with the wrong sort of people—one cannot be too careful in China, you know!"

"Yes, I know," said Forsythe grimly. "Did he say anything to you about gambling?"

"Yes; his last evening here," she replied gravely. "He left early—he was going to meet some friends and visit a gambling house in the Chinese City. We begged him to stay here, for we Russians are gamblers, you know, and we play among ourselves; but he insisted on leaving. And the next day he was dead. Ah, but it is terrible! If I had only known! A few thousand dollars might have saved his life."

The technique, Forsythe decided, was none too good, but interesting.

"Well," he said, rising, "I must get along; didn't realize how late it was. I'm mighty sorry to have bothered you, princess, and I'm glad that Van found such good friends here. You see, I want to write his folks about it, and they'll be tickled to know that he was running around with nobility."

"But you are not leaving, now?" she protested in surprise.

"I guess I'd better," and Forsythe smiled. "I'm at the hotel, and I've got to find me a room somewhere; I don't like hotels. Haven't even unpacked my clothes yet. If I—"

"Wait!" She lifted her hand. "You are free this evening—you will come here and dine at eight? We shall welcome you. Any friend of poor Vanessen is our friend! I want you to meet our little circle here. We live quietly, it is true, but I like Americans, me! You do not speak French?"

Forsythe grinned. "Nope, I'll have to learn French and Chinese, I expect, but there's lots of time for that before I grow old."

"Then you must let me give you French lessons!" she exclaimed with vivacity. "And I think we may be able to find room for you here, too, if you'd care to come. You know, this is a very large place, and a number of my friends live here; we Russians have little money, and we club together. Perhaps we can arrange it—"

SIX EVENINGS later beheld Forsythe very differently situated.

He sat in his upstairs room in the villa of the princess—a small but comfortable room—and awaited his caller, General Bougdanov, one of the little group of Russians domiciled here. He knew exactly what the call would bring forth, and smiled through his cigarette smoke.

"They're taking no chances of anything going wrong this time," he reflected complacently. "They've got me installed here. I'm about five thousand dollars to the bad, and everything's ready for the blowoff—whatever that may be. They must be in a hurry, too, the way they've worked it! They probably had worked along with Vanessen, grooming him for the job, and his suicide pretty near knocked them cold. Hm! Somebody's going to pay for that, too."

His eyes were bleak and grim as he thought about it. He knew now that Princess Orloff was merely a pretty bait, a secondary personage in this game of intrigue. The real bellwether of the pack was Bougdanov; and diplomacy, so-called, was somehow involved. Here at this house Forsythe had met one or two attachés of legations, a consul from Mukden, several sleek agents of the war lords, and the local branch manager of the Hongkong Commercial Bank; but nowhere had he been able to pick up any hint of what was in the wind.

Seven thirty. Dinner in half an hour—

Bougdanov knocked and entered. The old general was in resplendent uniform, white whiskers brushed back, features vigorous and rosy; years were nothing to his vitality. He bowed ceremoniously and accepted the chair offered by Forsythe.

"My friend," he said solemnly, in his excellent English, as he patted Forsythe paternally on the knee, "I like you. And you know the old man he will help you, eh? Now, look; I have taken up every I O U which you have given."

Forsythe's amazement was very real. Bougdanov produced those chits, so liberally handed out by a willing victim, and rapidly totalled them up.

"Over five thousand of your American dollars, eh?" His little eyes twinkled. "That is a lot of money, my young friend! You cannot pay. It means disgrace, eh? It is bad business. You have played heavily, unwisely. Well, fear not! I shall help you."

He leaned back and produced cigarettes. Forsythe struck a match.

"It's mighty good of you, general," he said huskily. "No, I couldn't meet those chits. I've been frantic. Desperate! And now I owe you all the money, is that it?"

"That is it," said Bougdanov. "But there is a favor you can do me. You can help me, and I will tear up these chits, you understand?"

"You mean it?" cried Forsythe. "I'll do anything, general! Anything except steal the money—"

"Pouf!" Bougdanov waved his cigarette, laughed heartily. "You will have your little joke, yes? Well, in three days you can earn that five thousand dollars. Good pay, eh? And all by doing me a favor. Listen! The other day I have drink too much, you understand? I have talked about my friend from America. To-night we have two guests. They do not speak English, but they wish to behold my American millionaire friend. You will take his name, act his part. Money is nothing to you. Whatever I say, you will say yes. You comprehend?"

"Eh? Is that all?" exclaimed Forsythe eagerly. He seized the general's hand. "Say, you bet I will! What's the name you want me to take?"

"Bayer." Bougdanov beamed upon him. "Robert Bayer. So, it is settled! You will be down presently for dinner, yes? Good. I like you, young man."

HE DEPARTED. Forsythe ditched the Russian cigarette and lit one of his own, thoughtfully.

Here was a clew, at least; but he could not see whither it led. The imposture appeared insensate and meaningless. Robert Bayer was the United States consul general at Mukden, with Manchuria and northern China under his eye.

Well, have to see later. A further clew might turn up with the two guests. So far, Mr. Forsythe had gleaned little through his knowledge of Chinese and French; when his friends talked among themselves they used Russian or German, both of which were closed books to him. So he eyed his evening clothes in the mirror with some distaste, pinched his tie into the right shape, and descended to dinner.

The guests were two stocky, peasant-faced Chinese in uniform; one a general, the other a colonel. With them was a third, a captain—a slim youngster who shook hands heartily with Forsythe and addressed him in slangy English. A Chinese from America, acting as interpreter for the other two. Forsythe saw now why only an American could have played this part.

The dinner was quietly brilliant. On the right of the princess were the three Chinese, on her left were Forsythe and Boug-danov. Two middle-aged Russian women, who said little or nothing, and the sallow secretary, whose name was Nieuhoff, completed the table. Presently Forsythe discovered that the Chinese had just arrived in Tientsin from the west.

"And how," queried Bougdanov, beaming upon the general, "is our good friend, General Fu?"

"He is well, and lives in hope," came the reply through the interpreter.

"All is arranged," said Bougdanov. "We shall discuss it later."

The dinner proceeded, and Forsythe had another clew. This Fu, of course, must be the great Fu Wei, defeated some months since, and who had given up dreams of conquest to become a student in a Buddhist monastery. In reality he was probably biding his time to make another descent upon his fellow war lords who had brought chaos and anarchy to all China.

With the liqueurs, the ladies left the room. Nieuhoff, whom Forsythe now suspected of being a partner with Bougdanov in the latter's entire scheme, dismissed the servants and closed the doors. The Chinese colonel spoke rapidly to the interpreter in his own tongue.

"Think you this foreign devil is the right man?"

"Undoubtedly," came the response. "He is certainly an American."

"Then handle the matter. Remember, no money is to be paid until we have the letter from the American President."

Bougdanov now turned to Forsythe, beamingly.

"My dear Bayer," he began, "you know the matter of which I spoke with you. Has it gained your approval or not?"

"Certainly it has," assented Forsythe, while the interpreter listened.

"And did you cable as I suggested?"

"Yes. I shall get a reply to-morrow or next day."

"Then you remain here? You will stop as our guest?"

Forsythe regarded him in obvious astonishment.

"What? Naturally I shall remain until this is settled! But as your guest—well, yes. I thank you, and shall be very glad of your hospitality."

Bougdanov was utterly delighted by Forsythe's words and air, which so thoroughly backed up his own game. The interpreter was putting the dialogue into Chinese. Bougdanov waited.

"And when," he asked, "do you think we may be sure of having an answer? It is necessary to arrange a meeting with these gentlemen, who, as you know, represent General Fu Wei."

Forsythe reflected. "Day after to-morrow, certainly."

So it was arranged. They rejoined the ladies, and business was taboo for the evening.

FORSYTHE LEFT in the morning for his supposed work without seeing Bougdanov again. He was still wholly in the dark regarding the game that was being played; while he might have wired the real Bayer at Mukden or communicated with the American consul here, he dared make no false move. An item in the *Times,* stating that Bayer was in Tientsin on consular business, puzzled him, but he took for granted that it had been inspired by Bougdanov.

Then, unexpectedly, everything broke at once.

It was four in the afternoon when Connor's manager hastily informed him that Bougdanov was outside. Connor cleared his desk hastily, donned his assumed spectacles, and a moment later looked up as the Russian entered. The old general was obviously excited.

"We can talk here, my friend?" he asked abruptly. "It is safe?"

Forsythe nodded and locked the door, then resumed his chair.

"Go ahead, general. What's on your mind?"

With an effort Bougdanov got himself under control.

"First," he said, "I must explain to you. Perhaps you know how important is the influence of America in China to-day? Well, General Fu Wei somehow came to believe that I might obtain for him the backing of America, if and when he returns to the stage of war. In fact, I am to receive a large sum in cash, a very large sum, if I obtain a letter from the American President and a statement from the consul general approving him and giving him recognition. Now do you comprehend?"

There it was in a nutshell—an astonishing, almost incredible scheme.

Forsythe nodded and lit a cigarette, hiding his impulse to laugh. A ridiculous thing, no doubt; yet it had cost the life of Vanessen already.

"I see," he replied. "I am to supply the letter or cable, and a statement; you get the money. Is that it?"

Bougdanov spread out his hands in a warning gesture.

"We are not dealing with fools, my friend!" he exclaimed. "Listen. Our plans have been made for a long time, but sometimes there are slips. For example, we must do the thing to-night, instead of to-morrow. I have already summoned our Chinese friends. To-night you will identify yourself to them; I shall then have everything ready for you—papers, letters, government records, everything! You will hand them a cablegram, make a statement which will be typed on the proper note paper; that is all. You comprehend?"

"And I make five thousand, eh?" said Forsythe, with a smile. "Excellent!"

The other rose, beaming. "Ah, young man, I like you! We dine simply, by ourselves; the Chinese do not arrive until nine. Before then, we shall make arrangements. You find the plan to your taste?" he added, a trifle anxiously. "You do not refuse?"

"Refuse? Do I look like a fool?" Forsythe broke into a laugh and went to the door, arm in arm with his visitor. "My dear general, it's a great little scheme! I only wish I'd thought of it in the first place!"

He ushered out the Russian, then hastened back to his desk and caught up the telephone. The words "note paper" had given him an idea. In three minutes he had the American consul in Tientsin on the line.

"Hello—Vincent Connor speaking," he said. "Oh, Japan? Sure, I started for there, but had to attend to some business.

Keep it quiet, will you? I wanted to learn whether your consul general in Mukden is here—he is? No, I don't want to see him, merely wanted to tip him off that something underhand seems to be going on. Stopping at your house, eh? All right, thanks. I may run over and see him in the morning. Good-by."

He hung up, frowning. "So that's that—and hanged if I can see why old Bougdanov was so excited! We'll have a genuine surprise for him to-night, perhaps."

It did not occur to him that Bougdanov might have a surprise for *him*.

WHEN FORSYTHE got home to the villa he saw no one but the French maid; the place seemed quite deserted.

He bathed leisurely, dressed with care, and under his arm-pit snuggled the small pistol in its shoulder-holster. By this time it was dark. The one window of his room opened above the villa's *porte-cochère*, and he had just switched off his lights, preparatory to descending, when he heard the strident hum of a car coming to a halt. He went to the window just in time to hear an altercation about a fare, and to see a taxicab drive away—a French Renault taxi, as the slope of the hood told him.

Something held him at his door—some vague restraint. He heard a subdued oath from the hall, and then the voice of Nieuhoff in rapid French.

"Into my room with him—safe enough there. You take charge of the portfolio."

A grunt in Bougdanov's voice made answer. Forsythe frowned. They were bringing some one; who, then? Perhaps one of their Russian friends was dead drunk. It had happened before this.

Presently Forsythe descended, found Princess Orloff in the library writing letters, and was not astonished at the lack of warmth in her manner. She had snared him, and her part was finished; indeed, he rather liked her coolness. He had already guessed that she was either the wife or mistress of Nieuhoff.

Bougdanov appeared, dressed for dinner, and very self-satisfied and complacent. Later Nieuhoff descended, just as dinner was served. Forsythe came to the conclusion that he had been unduly on the alert—when, as Nieuhoff lifted an arm, he saw a distinct splotch of red on the man's wrist above his cuff.

Dinner over, Bougdanov glanced at his watch, then looked at Forsythe.

"Come, my friend! We have just time to make arrangements."

Obediently, the American followed him into the library. On the large center table was an opened brief case, with papers strewn around it. Forsythe took the chair at the table, and Bougdanov handed him a cablegram, properly filled out.

"Here is the cablegram from the President, my friend. Nieuhoff is now preparing the statement which you will sign, in presence of our guests. Do you think you can carry it off?"

"Of course," said Forsythe, glancing over the cabled message, and laying it down. "These other papers—look here, general! They look pretty genuine, and I see Bayer's name on that *portefeuille*. Why not bring in your yellow friends and leave them here for two or three minutes? Never fear, they'll do their own examining of these papers!"

Bougdanov rubbed his hands, and then pawed his white whiskers, beamingly.

"Good! Admirable! You have a head, my friend."

Forsythe rose, pocketing the false cablegram.

"I'll run up to my room—they'll be here any moment now. Tell 'em I'm just getting the cablegram now—anything you like."

He hurried from the room. As he passed through the salon he saw Nieuhoff busily working over a typewriter, Princess Orloff looking over his shoulder at the work. Forsythe went on quickly, unobserved. He was suddenly afraid of what he might find. That man they had fetched in from the taxicab—

Perhaps from haste, perhaps thinking such precaution needless, Nieuhoff had left the door of his room unlocked. Forsythe entered, closed the door again, switched on the lights. Upon the bed lay a man, well-trussed, blood upon his face. He was unconscious.

FORSYTHE FELL to work, cutting the cords that bound the man—he must be Bayer—mopping his face with a wet towel. Upon this discovery, everything was changed. What had seemed a game of childish proportions, based upon the almost unbelievable credulity of men, now assumed darker aspects. Here was not graft alone, but actual crime. That faked cablegram from the President, that statement with the signature of the consul general, would be ultimately disproved; meantime, incalculable damage would be wrought to the prestige of the United States. Their plan was to keep Bayer out of the way for a few days, probably—

The eyes of the man on the bed came open.

"Quiet, Bayer, quiet!" Forsythe was working rapidly, bandaging the deep cut above the ear. "Do nothing, or you're lost! Do you understand me?""

"Yes," murmured the other, staring at him. "But who are you?"

"Never mind. No time to talk now. Lie here and get your strength back; you'll be safe enough until I return. I'll get you out of here somehow."

"My brief case!" Bayer made a convulsive movement, which Forsythe repressed with strong hands. "The trade agreement with Manchuria—with the Japanese—"

"I'll get everything," Forsythe assured him. "Listen! Obey me, or the whole game is up. Understand? Lock the door of this room. Don't open it unless I tap three times, or unless you hear a shot. Use your head, old man, and depend on me."

"But who—"

"Never mind now. Get that door locked as soon as I'm out. See you later."

With this, Forsythe slipped swiftly from the room and went to his own room at the end of the hall. Barely had he switched on the lights and given his dress tie a twitch when he heard the heavy tread of Bougdanov, who appeared in the doorway.

"Come! They are here—"

"Right."

Together they descended to the salon, where the princess was talking with Nieuhoff. The latter turned and extended a typed document to Forsythe.

"Here you are!" he exclaimed. "Sign this, read it to them—that is all!"

With a nod, Forsythe pocketed the document, typed on the official stationery of the consulate general. All three of them went on to the library; after them floated the voice of Princess Orloff in a soft *"bon chance!"*

Then Forsythe found himself exchanging bows and handgrips with the Chinese general and colonel, while the captain-interpreter grinned.

"Pray be seated, gentlemen," said Forsythe, assuming his own chair before the papers and open brief case. "Unfortunately, I have an appointment in half an hour, so let's get to business. I have here a cablegram. Shall I read it to you? Better, captain, that you put it into Chinese."

He handed the cablegram to the interpreter, who read to his delighted superiors the very flattering phrases, supposedly sent by the President of the United States, and his assurances that General Fu Wei would receive the unlimited support and backing of America. The audacity of the thing drew a gasp from Forsythe, who had not read the message.

"We may keep this cable?" inquired the interpreter. Forsythe waved his hand.

"By all means. And here is my own statement."

H E D R E W forth the typed document, and the interpreter proceeded to read this also. Bougdanov pawed his whiskers and beamed approval; Nieuhoff listened attentively, his sallow features tensed. Forsythe, now prepared for anything, heard the smooth assurances of the consul general that General Fu Wei would be supported by the United States, that his claims to the overlordship of all China would be recognized, and so forth.

The Chinese general and colonel were delighted beyond words, as their glittering eyes testified.

"There is no doubt in this matter," said the interpreter in rapid dialect to the other two. "You see this embossed note paper. You have seen the other documents. This is more than we had hoped for, indeed."

"It is sufficient," returned the general, and his colleague nodded. "It must be signed."

Forsythe took the typed sheet, opened the brief case, and found a proper envelope. Nieuhoff extended a fountain pen. Forsythe tested it, signed the statement, and blotting it, folded and placed it in the envelope. Bougdanov rose.

"One moment," he said to the interpreter. "I believe there is a stipulation—"

The general produced a wallet, and from it took a cashier's check on the Yokohama Specie Bank. Bougdanov passed it to Nieuhoff, whose eyes dilated greedily.

"It is safe enough," he said in French. "They may, of course, stop it, but will have no valid reason; besides, we will cash it first thing in the morning."

Forsythe remained, gathering up the scattered documents and replacing them in the brief case. He found Nieuhoff eying him with narrowed, speculative gaze.

"You may leave those things here," said the Russian.

"Very well." Forsythe rose. Nothing else for it now—he had hoped to avoid force, but knew that these documents must be saved for Bayer. "Have you a cigarette?"

The other extended his case, and he took a tube. Nieuhoff closed the case and pocketed it—and as he did so, Forsythe's fist swung up.

The short-arm jab jolted Nieuhoff backward off balance. Before he could recover or even cry out, Forsythe's left slammed into the angle of his jaw. He crashed backward and lay still. Forsythe paused to light his cigarette, glanced down at the quiet figure, then caught up the brief case and left the room.

No one was in the salon; the Chinese visitors were being ceremoniously ushered from the house. Forsythe took the stairs two at a time, saw nobody, came to Nieuhoff's door, and tapped the agreed signal. There was no response. The door was locked. Impatient, dismayed, Forsythe drew back and flung his weight upon the door. At the second try, it crashed down.

The lighted room was empty, the window open.

In a flash he perceived that Bayer, probably fearing some further trap, had taken his chance of escape. Crossing to the window, he looked out. Directly below was the flat roof of the garage—and he beheld a dark figure just swinging to the ground.

"Bayer!" His voice reached out urgently. "Wait for me!"

A rush of footsteps, a wild oath—he looked back over his shoulder to see Nieuhoff in the doorway, reaching hand to pocket. Tossing the brief case from the window, Forsythe swung around. The little pistol leaped out into his hand, just as Nieuhoff's weapon came clear.

The two shots blended together.

An instant later, unharmed, Forsythe dropped to the garage roof, found the brief case, and gained the ground. Bayer caught him as he stumbled.

"All right? Good. Come along."

Five minutes afterward, in the wide Avenue Kléber, Forsythe waved down a passing taxicab and pushed Bayer into the vehicle.

"The Tientsin Club, *mon ami.*"

"Look here!" protested Bayer. "I want to go—"

"You're going with me," said Connor, and gave his own name. "No great damage has been done except to your skull—unless my shot finished Nieuhoff, which I don't think. What we need is a drink and a talk, and we'll get it."

GET IT they did, in Connor's rooms, while he swiftly worked getting rid of his mustache and sideburns, and into his own clothes. He talked as he worked, giving Bayer the entire story.

"So you see," he concluded, "no harm's been done—"

"No harm? Good Lord, man!" exclaimed Bayer in dismay. "Don't you realize that those Chinese will start their propaganda at once, that the United States will be dragged in—"

"Nope." Connor gave him a quizzical smile. "They won't do anything of the sort. They'll either jump on that gang good and hard, or keep quiet. My guess is that before to-morrow morning poor Vanessen's death will be avenged, the check will be taken back or payment stopped; and the whole gang will be in a bad hole all around."

"But why?" demanded Bayer, staring. "With my name signed to that statement, on our own official paper—"

Connor chuckled. "It wasn't," he said. "No one looked to see what name I signed. As a matter of fact, I signed none. I merely wrote the words 'Go to hell' and folded the paper."

Connor and his guest were at breakfast next morning when they heard the news. It was brought, in fact, by Connor's general manager.

"Of the most interesting, perhaps," he said, his sleek Chinese face wrinkled with smiles. "But of the most sad, also. An old man, General Bougdanov, seriously hurt, his friend M. Nieuhoff killed, Princess Orloff prostrated—"

"What!" exclaimed Connor. "Who did it?"

"Nobody knows, Mr. Connor. Robbers entered their villa just at dawn."

With a bow, the Chinese departed. Connor looked at Bayer, and grinned.

"What did I tell you, eh? I guess they've paid up for Vanessen! And," he added, "I will say he was right about one thing— she was a nifty blonde!"

III

THE TOMB-ROBBER

All China was buzzing with talk about the theft of the priceless Han jades when Connor, free lance of Oriental politics, took a hand in the risky game.

CONNOR WAS dining with the British consul when he first heard the name. D'Estrees, the French *attaché*, brought up the topic.

"I understand that chap Soper has sent a lot of his stuff this way. Any one heard of it?"

A general negative, and Connor asked who Soper might be.

"He's the tomb-robber. Joined with that bandit over beyond Lu-wan, and they've been robbing all the tombs of the Han emperors. Beastly shame, I call it. China has respected those tombs for two thousand years."

"Yes," said some one, "but I hear that some marvelous loot was obtained—priceless stuff."

"Just who is this Soper?" asked Connor again. "A Chinese?"

"Nobody knows. Adventurer of some sort, perhaps Russian, perhaps English. They say he had stuff at Shanghai worth millions. Some patriotic Chinese down there have tried to buy it, I understand, but failed. Don't know why. Perhaps this chappie asked too much."

"He'd better offer it to Connor, here," said some one, amid a general laugh. "Connor has the money to buy it, and we'd all chip in and start a museum."

"Museum my eye!" said the consul. "Auction it in London—— whew! Fortunes in it. Better cast a hook out, Connor. Get hold of the stuff."

"Thanks," said Connor coolly. "I will."

47

"I want the jades," snapped Rhodes.

To the foreign colony, at least, Connor was a pleasant but negligible quantity. He lived at the Tientsin Club; he had inherited great business interests extending over half China; he played polo and enjoyed life in a non-serious manner. Nobody, in fact, took Vincent Connor very seriously, among his social acquaintances.

There were others, however, who did. Others, who did not count in the social whirl, but who counted heavily enough in other ways. One of these was old Chang, who had been the partner of Connor's father, and who from his retirement in Shanghai kept his finger very closely upon the pulse of China. More than once, strange coincidences had occurred, and when he got home to his rooms at the club this same evening, Connor was not surprised to find upon his table a special delivery letter from Shanghai.

In the neat ideographs used by Chang was a message which Connor swiftly translated:

The despoiler of the dragon-throne has come and gone. Honorable purchase of the Han *yu* is refused. It would be a meritorious action were the robber to be robbed before he brings shame upon the sons of Han and sells the Lu-wan silver mines to the Roman syndicate.

Connor could picture the old man brushing these characters in a sort of savage contempt, writing a cryptic message which, unless Connor could read its import, would mean nothing. And if it had not been for the conversation at dinner, Connor might have studied it in vain.

As it was, he had the clew. Soper the mysterious was probably headed for Tientsin or might be here now, with a collection of jade from the Han tombs—and Han *yu* is precious stuff, since it disappeared from Chinese markets centuries ago. The final sentence, however, was rather startling. Soper, who with his bandit partner held the Lu-wan district firmly grasped, meant to use the jade to help sell the concession to the Lu-wan silver mines, among the richest in China—to the Romans! Then Connor realized that this ideograph must mean Italians. That threw a new light on the whole affair.

Here, then, was a point of departure!

HE WENT to his office the next morning, thoughtfully. There was a matter under dispute with the Italian consul—a question of arbitrary rental increases on godowns leased by the Connor interests. Calling up the consulate, he gained a speedy appointment and was presently on his way thither.

As with all Fascist officials, he found himself dealing with a man who was adamant, who regarded the dispute with an eye to strict justice, and who proposed an accord which Connor promptly accepted, knowing he would get nothing better. His business finished, he rose and then paused.

"By the way, we gained a concession six months ago on the two silver mines near the Yunnan border, in the Lao country. We've decided not to do anything about it at present, on account of the chaotic conditions down there, but I understand that an

Italian syndicate is going into that field. We do not desire any competition, and if you can tell me the proper person to see, it would be to our mutual advantage, I'm sure."

"Yes?" The consul regarded his visitor keenly, then nodded. "I understand such a syndicate is contemplated, but I know nothing about it officially. I suspect that Cavaliere Biencamino is interested—he is in Tientsin now—and you might see him."

"Thank you," said Connor. "And his address?"

The official searched his desk, opened a notebook which had been at his elbow all the while, and found that the Cavaliere was the guest of the Italia Line agent.

Connor departed, well satisfied; a little bait had caused the hook to be taken. Now he knew the man to see—the man whom Soper would be dealing with. And he knew that Biencamino and his syndicate would have the actual, if unofficial, backing of Italy. Therefore, a good deal more than mere jade or silver concessions was at stake, and shrewd old Chang had known it all the while.

Reflection told Connor that the only means of reaching the mysterious Soper lay through this Cavaliere Biencamino and the golden bait. His concession on the two silver mines was perfectly valid, but according to Chinese law one-half the stock in the company had to be Chinese-owned; it was of course held by old Chang. Within an hour, Connor held a telegraphed agreement giving one Wang Erh Yu an option on Chang's stock at par for thirty days; he also had an option on the Connor stock, for the same period, made out to the same Mr. Wang.

"We'll have to call the old bungalow into service," he reflected, and reached for the telephone. Speaking in Chinese, he called the Italia Line, got the agent's comprador, and gave the name of Wang Erh Yu. He professed an ability to speak French, and in five minutes had hooked his fish. The Cavaliere was on the line.

"I am a retired financier of Yunnan, honorable sir," he said, "and I have just secured complete control, or an option on same, of two silver mines near the Lao district. From the Connor interests. I should like very much to have a talk with you, but unfortunately my health does not permit me to go abroad. If I might send my car for you, and if you would do me the honor or dining with me at my home, I should be very gratified. We might find the evening mutually profitable."

Biencamino hesitated. "May I call you in half an hour?"

"Certainly," said Connor, and gave the number of his own private telephone. He called in his general manager.

"In ten minutes an Italian gentleman will telephone asking about that option on the silver mines. Give him full information about Wang Erh Yu—wealthy, young, underground political connections in the south, and so forth. Make it strong."

Almost to the minute, his prediction was fulfilled. His grinning manager was telling him of the conversation, when his private telephone rang. Biencamino was on the line.

"M. Wang? I shall accept your invitation with pleasure. At what hour?"

"I'll send my car for you at a few minutes to eight, if that is convenient—"

"Thank you."

Connor chuckled and called another number—that of the so-called bungalow, in reality a viceroy's pleasure palace he had inherited from his father. He seldom used it, but the old family number one boy kept it up.

"This you, Hung?" he said. "Good. A dinner for two at eight, European style. Have all the rooms lighted and everything on display. Send the little Austin for me at seven—I'll be at the club. Serve that special Lacrimæ Cristi, the Château Roger '16, and Chartreuse. And use the silver service."

For half an hour he studied a large-scale map, checked off certain properties owned or leased by the Connor interests, and then knocked off work for the day.

AT SEVEN Connor left the Tientsin Club in the tiny car;

he was, as usual, the acme of sartorial perfection. Fifteen minutes later, in his dressing-room at the bungalow, he underwent a transformation. A saffron tincture subtly altered his healthy bronze to a yellowish hue. Grease coarsened and thickened his black hair. His wide-angled, pleasant features were deftly altered by plugs of cotton which widened his nostrils and changed the set of his lips; a touch or two of collodion gave his lids an oblique effect, while his blue eyes peered forth owlishly from behind black-rimmed spectacles. Garments of a deftly awkward cut completed the costume of Mr. Wang Erh Yu, and he was ready when his guest arrived.

Cavaliere Biencamino was a tall, sturdy man from the north of Italy, with crisp yellow hair, alert eyes, a heavy jaw, and an air of resolute intelligence; at all points a dangerous antagonist. He was in his early forties, spoke French fluently, and from the moment of his entry was obviously impressed by the stage set to receive him. And small wonder.

Any one would have been impressed by the luxury both Oriental and Occidental of this stone palace with beams and pillars of *nanmu* wood, fragrant after two hundred years. The walls were hung with silk tapestries of imperial yellow, and the floor was covered by rugs that had been part of the glories of Hang Hi's reign. The dining room glimmered with Georgian silver and the rarest glass, and the lamps on the table were of golden *cloisonné* from the Summer Palace; the dinner was faultless, the service was perfect.

Mr. Wang, however, scarcely tasted the food, pleading his health. He had already dined at the club, for with his facial disguise he dared take no chances. With the coffee and liqueur he broached the topic of business, and found the Cavaliere a ready listener. All Mr. Wang desired was to get rid of those silver mines without taking a loss, and for the Italian it was a profitable stroke of business. This arranged tentatively, Mr. Wang went on smoothly to what he chiefly wanted, picking up some incidental information as to the Italian syndicate.

"You would be interested, perhaps, in coal fields near Lu-wan?" he asked. "Or even in the merest of political influence in the south? My health forces me to live simply, yet I am not entirely destitute of ability to serve my friends. As you see, I live the life of a collector, surrounding myself with beautiful objects eloquent of China's past history."

As he paused, the Italian eyed him speculatively and then asked:

"Are you by any chance acquainted with a M. Rhodes, an American?"

Mr. Wang smiled, placed a cigarette between his rather full lips, and lighted it. He knew instantly that he was now on Soper's trail.

"Very well indeed," he said blandly, in singsong French which Biencamino could understand only with some, difficulty. "It was I who started him and his partner upon his very prosperous career. However," he added, "you will understand when I say that I did not then use the family name of Wang. And, in leaving the south, I also left my assumed identity behind me."

"I see," murmured the Italian thoughtfully. He eyed the cups in which the Chartreuse was served—tiny cups carven with hydra heads. He fingered his own cup. "Beautiful jade, this—I have rarely seen this yellow shade. Han jade, of course."

"You are a collector?" queried Mr. Wang.

"Well, it interests me," returned the other cautiously. "Do you happen to know of the project which M. Rhodes now has under way?"

"Unfortunately, no," said Mr. Wang. "I understand he has some fine tomb relics,"

"So I hear. Hm! There is a possibility that he may soon be in Tientsin. Would you care to meet him again?"

"With all my heart!" Mr. Wang's cordiality was by no means assumed. He now knew that Rhodes was the real name of the mysterious Soper. "If I might have the honor of arranging that he be supplied with a guest-card by the Tientsin Club—"

"*Per Baccho!* The very thing!" exclaimed the Italian. Then he frowned. "But I understood that no Chinese are members?"

"I will arrange it with M. Connor. You know him, perhaps? An idle young man."

The other nodded. "I've heard of him. Too much money for his own good, eh? By all means, M. Wang! This will be very good of you. Perhaps the three of us might have a talk, eh? Let me see—he gets here to-morrow night from, Shanghai—hm! Shall we say, a meeting on Friday?"

"Agreed," said Mr. Wang heartily. "Telephone me at any time as to the hour."

He saw his guest off, returned to his own identity, and got back to the club in the nick of time to join in a rubber of auction.

HE HAD learned a good deal: who Soper really was; that he would arrive from Shanghai the next evening, when a China Merchants' boat was due in; also, he was not to be the guest of Biencamino—probably was to avoid any contact with the Italian in public. An even more important point, perhaps; he had learned that Cavaliere Biencamino was a collector. Although the Italian had scarcely admitted it, the glint in his eyes had been eloquent.

"Hm! Rhodes is bribing him with that tomb jade," thought Connor. "Something worth more than the cash sum Chang offered for the jade. Can't figure it out, but there's a fishy smell to it. Devilish fishy smell! Old Chang suspected it, but had no proof."

Neither had Connor any proof, but he meant to get it.

Having no doubt that Rhodes would jump at the chance to stop at the Tientsin Club, he arranged to have a guest-card sent out to the incoming steamer by the pilot boat, with his compliments, and then made careful arrangement at the club as to the rooms Rhodes would be given if he arrived. This done, he visited his own consulate and from the consul made guarded inquiries as to Rhodes.

"Haven't heard of the chap in a year or more," said the consul.

"Bad record, though; hope he doesn't turn up here to make trouble. Eh?"

"I think he will," said Connor lazily. "Just how is he bad? I have business interests—"

"Then keep your eye peeled," came the blunt warning. "Look out for bad checks, confidence games, anything! The fellow has left a nasty trail. Don't mix up with him."

"Thanks very much," said Connor, and departed.

Rhodes had been out of sight for a year, playing the rôle of Soper. Now he had a big thing on hand, and would push it hard, to the exclusion of everything else; it must be big indeed, if he had turned down a flat cash offer from Chang, who was no piker. Pondering the matter, Connor reluctantly determined that only one course was open to him. Accordingly, he made inquiries as to the landing hour of the Shanghai boat, and then waited to see if the dice would fall his way. The chances were against him. However, Biencamino's eagerness at the idea of the Tientsin Club made it likely that he would send Rhodes thither. And the adventurer would possibly have the gall to accept the idea, though he must know that warnings had been broadcast against him.

AT NINE that evening, Connor was strolling about the club lobby, idly chatting with one man and another, when the dice fell double six. A tall, lean, bronzed man entered, the boys fetching in half a dozen suitcases and kit-bags after him. He walked to the desk with a swift, nervous stride; Connor studied him covertly and knew his man had come. The keen, predatory features, the thin lips and arrogant eyes, the military swing of the shoulders, all told their story. When the new arrival had gone to his room, Connor sauntered over and spoke with the manager.

"Yes—Rhodes," said the latter. "He presented the card from you."

"Right. And the room?"

"As arranged, Mr. Connor."

With a nod, Connor turned away. Now to see if his calculations would come out aright!

Twenty minutes, he had told himself; he was only two minutes wrong. Eighteen minutes, indeed, after entering, Rhodes reappeared and summoned a taxicab. Connor turned to the elevator and went at once to his own room. The one which had been given Rhodes was on the same floor and only three doors away.

"He's gone to see Biencamino, of course," thought Connor, switching on his lights. "That means I've half an hour to work, perhaps more."

On his dresser lay a key, made for him the same afternoon. He picked it up, stepped out into the corridor, and a moment later paused before the door of Rhodes's room. The key fitted. As he had anticipated, the array of suitcases were all locked; he studied them, lifted them. Three were exactly alike, very heavy, and new—obviously purchased for the trip. Selecting one of these, he attacked the back of it with the razor he had brought along, and cut out a large segment.

A moment later, he was lifting out the jade of the Han emperors.

With brush and ink-slab Connor carefully sketched the proper ideograms on a sheet of paper, which he deposited inside the uppermost of the three emptied suitcases; he guessed that Rhodes could read them or have them read. The message was simple:

> The imperial ancestors have taken back what was stolen from their tombs. At noon to-morrow I will telephone you.

Locking the door of Rhodes's room, he regained his own apartment, leaving the door slightly ajar. He turned back the spread of his bed, and upon the blankets laid out the jades, which he had taken from their wrappings. Here was the most magnificent lot of Han jade he had ever seen at one time— yellow, brown, black, mottled. The scarabs which had reposed on the tongues of emperors were exquisitely carved, and nearly all the larger pieces bore inscriptions; these last Connor placed in his closet.

H E WA S engaged in trying to sort out the various funerary sets—the mass of jade quite covered his bed—when he heard rapid steps in the hall. He drew the spread over the blankets and bits of stone, and went to the door, listening. Presently he heard a sharp cry, then a veritable explosion of oaths. He stepped out into the hall, and saw Rhodes at the door of his room, peering about.

"I beg your pardon," said Connor. "Anything wrong?"

"Yes! That is, no," returned Rhodes. "My room's been entered!"

"Oh, I say! Nothing's taken, I hope?"

"Everything's taken," said the other bitterly.

"Really? Here, old chap, come over to my room—Connor's the name. We'll have the club manager up and get out the police. Very efficient police here, you know. That's why we have the club in the British Concession; I'm one of the governors. Come along over."

"Connor, did you say?" Rhodes put out his hand. "I must thank you, then, for my guest-card. I'm Harrington Rhodes."

"Delighted, I'm sure." Connor flung open his door. "We'll have a drink, what? And get the manager and the police—"

"Not so fast," said Rhodes, entering. He had taken the blow like a man, and that alert, predatory face was now keen and tensed, coping with the problem. "A drink by all means, old man, but easy on the calls for aid. Nothing of much value was taken, and I'm not a bit anxious to kick up a row."

"Well, make yourself comfortable while I get a drink. High-balls?"

Rhodes nodded, and Connor went to the tantalus in the corner. He could well understand that Rhodes did not want the police brought in—indeed, he had counted upon this prob-ability. While the man might argue his title to the jades, explanations would be unpleasant, and undue publicity might be unpleasant also; for all China of the better class resented most acutely the looting of the ancient tombs, which had somehow crept into the press.

Rhodes—or Soper—eyed his host speculatively, and sipped his drink.

"No, nothing of much value gone," he said, and smiled. His smile was unpleasant; it was not unlike a grimace. "One or two trinkets left in sight—should have known better. By the way, how did you happen to send me that card? I've never met you before, to my knowledge."

"One of my business clients, a Mr. Wang, requested it, and I was very glad to be of any service to you," explained Connor. The other nodded. "Are you just out from home?"

Rhodes smiled at that. "I've been out for a bit," he said. "No griffin, at any rate. Are you the Connor with all the up-country interests? Heard of your firm down south. You're in timber and mines rather heavily, eh?"

"More or less, yes. Other lines as well. By the way, if I can be of any service to you about here, call upon me by all means. Some fair racing to-morrow; I have a couple of entries. If you care for racing—"

"Thanks, but I'm here on business and haven't much time."

Rhodes stayed out his drink, and then departed, and Connor was forced to admire the man's coolness. Then, as he was un-dressing, and before he had cleared the bed, Connor suddenly paused as though something had frozen him.

On the floor just under the edge of the bed lay a mottled yellow circlet—a figure of the earth-deity, that had slipped to the floor. Connor slowly picked it up and placed it with the other jades. Had Rhodes seen it there? He decided not. The adventurer would have taken fire on the instant, would have forced a show-down.

"I want the show-down myself," thought Connor. "I'll call him to-morrow noon, play Wang Erh Yu again, and settle him."

WITH WHICH resolution he went to bed and slept until seven, when he arose. He carefully packed the jades in two large suitcases of his own, called up two boys from below, and had the grips sent off to old Chang, in Shanghai. Then he went virtuously to breakfast.

At eleven that morning he was getting the last of his mail cleaned up when he was apprised that a Mr. Rhodes was waiting to see him. A moment later Rhodes strode into his private office, looking very fresh and fit.

"Morning, Connor!" said the adventurer cordially. "Busy?"

"Not a bit," said Connor. "How about the polo match this afternoon? We're taking on that team from the Punjab Light Horse, up from Hongkong. Should be good."

Rhodes nodded. "Thanks. Can do, perhaps. I really dropped in to ask if you'd do me a favor, old chap. I may be here for a bit, and I struck a chap this morning with two polo ponies he wants to sell. Looks like a ripping bargain, but I'm not a great judge of horseflesh, and I gather you know your way around. Besides, this chap is a Mongolian and I'm not sure of the interpreter—"

"Sure, sure!" assented Connor. "You want to watch out for these Mongols, though. Their horses are used to pasture, and go all to pieces on regular feed. Want to run out now?"

"If you like," said Rhodes. "I've a hired car waiting. This chap has his animals at a farm just outside town, and seems a suspicious sort. Regular wild animal himself."

"Some of them are," said Connor. "Be ready in half a minute."

Rhodes scrolled about, glancing at the pictures on the walls, and in five minutes Connor had finished his work and was ready. The car was a powerful Daimler, with a slant-eyed driver at the wheel.

Like most of his ilk, Rhodes could be a most attractive talker when he so desired, and Connor, plying him with questions about the chaotic political condition in the south, hardly noticing whither they were going, until they were out of the city. Then, with some surprise, he recognized the road.

"You can't get far along here with a car," he exclaimed. "As I recall, it's only a hill trail after that abandoned Kwannin shrine."

"That's as far as we'll go," said Rhodes carelessly. "It's just past there—we're nearly at the shrine now."

So they were, indeed, and not having been along this way for months, Connor ventured no protest. Presently the car halted, where a washout had ended that road for automobiles, and on their left, amid its grove of trees, showed the old and ruinous shrine to Kwannin. Rhodes got out, and motioned.

"Mind walking over there?" he asked. "I'd like to take a look at it."

Connor assented; though somewhat puzzled, he had no thought of danger. They came to the shrine—a little temple of but two rooms—and on the steps, Rhodes paused. Two ragged Chinese appeared in the entrance, and Connor addressed them.

"What are you doing here?"

"Waiting for you, venerable ancestor," said one, with a grin. Connor felt something touch his side, and turned. He found Rhodes there, eyes narrowed, pistol thrust against him.

"Inside, Connor," came the crackling command. "We'll do our talking there. And if you try any trouble, you'll get a bullet in your gizzard—so watch out!"

CONNOR WAS forced to an unwilling admiration of his host's thoroughness and speed. The inner room of the shrine had but one opening—the entrance door. Roofless walls rose high. Here a cot, two stools and a light table were placed in readiness for the guest. Connor looked at the two ragged men, whom Rhodes in Cantonese ordered to remain at the door; they were flat-faced Cantonese, obviously, and now each held a pistol as he lolled there.

Rhodes dropped on a stool and faced Connor.

"Come across, now," he demanded in a tone that meant business. Connor smiled.

"In what way? And what's all this melodrama about?"

"Never mind the funny stuff; put your cards on the table," snapped Rhodes. "I saw that jade disk by your bed last night. Where's the rest of it?"

"Where you won't get it." Connor lighted a cigarette and relaxed. "Not a bit of use, Soper, not a bit! Your luck has turned against you."

"Yeah? You may change your mind." The other snarled, showing his teeth. "Where's that jade? Want me to burn your feet?"

"Wouldn't do you any good," drawled Connor. "That jade's started half across China and I couldn't get it back if I wanted to. So just dismiss that entirely. You stole it from China, and China's taken it back."

The steely, merciless eyes bored into him. Rhodes was white about the lips with rage.

"Who told you about it?"

Connor smiled. "My dear chap, who do you suppose told me about it? The same person who told me how and when you were arriving, and about the deal for the Lu-wan mines, and so on."

He read a flash of doubt in the adventurer's face. Rhodes evidently felt none too sure of Biencamino, the Italian. But his uncertainty was only for a moment.

"Impossible!"

Connor shrugged. "As you like. Now, why not look at the facts in the case? I took your jades, granted; not for myself, but for China. No one will profit by them; no one should. And the same with your mining deal. If you'll put your cards on the table, I'll do the same, and you may find it better to work with me than against me."

"You be damned!" said Rhodes. "Hm! That devil Wang is mixed up in this somehow. I knew right off there'd be trouble if a chink mixed in!"

"So you think Biencamino would not double-cross you?" inquired Connor. The other stared hard at him.

"Is that it? Then—"

"Listen to me, Rhodes, or Soper, or whatever you want to call yourself." In Connor's voice was a sudden change, a bite of authority that held the other's attention. "You've a big game on hand; I don't know all the details. However, you'll find your game spoiled. Biencamino has arranged with Wang Erh Yu to take over some mines and other properties. I can still stop that. No one else can. Tell me just what you propose. If I want to throw in with you, all right; if not, no great harm's done."

"By George, you're a cool devil!" said Rhodes. "Who'd have thought a chap like you would assay so high? But you've barged into the wrong game, Connor. Not a soul knows where you are, and—hm! Might make you pay high, one way or another, I suppose."

He puffed at his cigarette, frowned, and finally nodded.

"Let's chance it. You know about the Italian syndicate? Right. They're taking over the Lu-wan mines, true, and a lot of other properties with them. In return, I get a big price for my jades—a hundred thousand gold and some syndicate stock."

"Wait a minute," intervened Connor. "Why the jades, anyway? You could have sold 'em down in Shanghai."

Rhodes grinned at him. "Don't you know Biencamino is a collector?"

"Uh-huh. What's behind it?"

"You're devilish shrewd, Connor. That jade is a bribe that goes to London—to the greatest collection in the world. See it now?"

Connor whistled. "Lord Southdown! And he's in the cabinet—"

"Will be, next election, when they chuck out the Labor Government. Italy wants a share of the trade pickings around down south, now that the central government is about smashed. The whole thing is cut and dried, Connor. Italy takes over these holdings and goes to work. I've been working with a Chinese partner down in those parts—"

"The bandit Liu Kun?"

"Exactly. He steps in, kills a few dagoes, grabs the properties—and Italy acts. Of course, without backing, she'd be rather helpless; hence, the jades. You see? England backs her play. Concessions no end, and so forth. Inside of five years, all that raw mineral wealth along the Yunnan border will be flowing into Italy. Great idea, eh? Money in it, too."

"How much do you want?" queried Connor. The other shook his head.

"You haven't enough. I want those jades."

"No can do. What's the alternative?"

"Sorry, Connor." Rhodes rose, his face like steel. "I don't believe you for a minute. There's no alternative. Either talk, or you'll be made to talk. Biencamino hasn't double-crossed me! Make up your mind. Hand back the jade, or by the Lord I'll burn every inch of your damned carcass from toes to head! We'll be back later. And you can't bribe those men. either. They've been with me for a year, and they know better than to gyp me. Try it if you like."

With his unpleasant smile, Rhodes departed.

THE AMERICAN heard the engine of the departing car, and reflected. He had no doubt whatever that Rhodes meant his words and would carry out his threat to the letter. Neither he nor the Italian would for a moment believe that Connor had sent away the jades—they had acted too swiftly for that, or so they would think.

Remembering the personality and manner of Biencamino, Connor could realize clearly that he was destined to suffer at the hands of that gentleman. He was, in fact, in a very tight pinch. He had fallen into his own trap; now neither brains nor guile would avail him, for he was dealing with men whose hard and ruthless habitude had pierced all his stratagems like iron breaking through soft ice.

"The penalty for mistakes," he thought bitterly. "Diploma-cy—save the mark!—isn't the thing here."

This was borne in upon him more fully when one of the two guards brought in some food and tea. Connor addressed him in Cantonese, and the man grinned.

"Honorable, if you attempt to bribe us, we must cut off your thumbs. That is the order."

An order that would be carried out; he could see it in the man's demeanor, and said no more.

Time dragged. The two Cantonese remained in the outer chamber of the shrine; from their voices, Connor concluded they were playing some game. He was unarmed—they had swiftly frisked him on entering the shrine. He examined the walls of the inner chamber with a critical eye; a snail might have climbed them, but nothing else, and they were fairly solid. That is, they seemed fairly solid, but the stone walls of old China merely filled in space and only carried their own weight—the principle of structural steel buildings, without the steel, was used a good many hundred years ago in the Middle Kingdom.

Connor saw sunlight through the rear wall, a hole the size of a walnut, and fell to work desperately. He knew that Rhodes and the Italian would not be long in getting here. So far, he concluded, Rhodes had been working alone, hoping to get back the jades at once. Even if he could get out of here, he knew, there was scant chance of escape, but he was not thinking of escape now. He was thinking of correcting his errors.

The hole grew. The ancient mortar was rotted and dead, the stones came out without too great trouble; presently he had a gap the size of his head, working only with the metal spoon that had accompanied his midday meal. He moved a stool before the hole and went back to the doorway of the outer room, cigarette in hand, and requested a light.

One of the guards accommodated him. It occurred to Connor that a thoroughgoing fictional hero would smack the man under the jaw, take his gun, and shoot the other guard; but viewed in cold blood, the plan had certain disadvantages—very practical ones. Connor hoped to gain the same end, and the gun, in a much safer manner. He knew enough of Chinese soldier-bandits to have a healthy respect for their weapons.

He loafed at the doorway, watched the guards resume their game, then went back to his own occupation. The hole was close to the floor, and swiftly increased in size. Somewhat to his own surprise, Connor presently put his foot against the edge and shoved out a square foot of the masonry. It would do now, he judged, and high time—Rhodes might be back at any moment. He looked through the hole. Outside was a drop of two feet to ground level.

CAREFULLY MOVING away the bamboo stool from before the opening, Connor turned and called out in Cantonese:

"Farewell, my friends! May good luck attend you."

On his hands and knees, he stooped, thrusting himself through the opening.

And as he emerged, he heard the sound of a motor approaching.

Pistol in hand, the first Cantonese came shoving through the ragged hole. Connor's rigid hand-edge struck the under side of his wrist a blow there, even if expected, relaxes or paralyzes the fingers. The pistol fell, and catching it, Connor dragged the man on through. The second man followed, stared into the barrel of the pistol, and dropped his own automatic.

Connor laughed as he regarded the pair of them, ragged and forlorn.

"Begone, sons of turtles! And thank the gods of luck."

They shambled away, grinning in defeat as they would have grinned while slicing off his hands.

Connor, tossing the two pistols through the hole, followed them back into the chamber.

Rhodes and Cavaliere Biencamino strode rapidly up to the

shrine and passed in the main entrance. Then they halted, blinking, as the command reached them.

"Hands up, gentlemen! Up—and empty, please!"

Rhodes, his keen, predatory features suddenly tensed, half lifted his hands. The Italian, with a voluble curse, shot his arms into the air. Then, desperation in his eyes, Rhodes took a catlike step behind his companion, hand diving to armpit like a snake for swiftness, gun flashing out.

Report after report crashed out within the stone walls, echoes reverberating thunderously, acrid smoke fumes drifting up. Blinded as they were in that dark chamber, the two men just in from the bright afternoon sunlight found their aim none too good. Stabbing fingers of flame shot out. Then silence, a single report, another.

Presently a figure came out of the doorway into the sunlight and halted.

Connor looked down at himself, started to brush the dirt from his white jacket, then looked out at the road's end. As he had thought, there was no driver now—Rhodes and the Italian had come alone.

"No, I'll have to walk back—wouldn't do to take the car in to town. Might be traced. As it is—the work of bandits."

He paused to light a cigarette, and smiled at sight of his trembling fingers.

"Well, my mistakes were rectified," he murmured. "And Rhodes, or Soper, made the most decided error of all. Odd! If he had only put up his bands. Well, he didn't. And his mistake was undeniably fatal. And poor Biencamino—by no means a bad sort—made the still more fatal mistake of interfering with China's destiny... I suppose now," and he glanced at the sun, "I'll miss that polo match, eh?"

And he turned toward the road. He had emerged from that chamber of death unscathed.

IV

DIPLOMACY BY AIR

Vincent Connor's political intrigues were so secret and successful that they puzzled all China; but this blow drove him to open and reckless action.

VINCENT CONNOR sat in the lounge of the Tientsin Club and stared dully at the telegram in his hand; the wording of it had knocked him into a chair. In more than one sense, the props were swept out from under him.

About him was the luxury of the club—uniformed boys, English and American business men nodding good morning to him, privately thinking him an idler who had inherited the Connor fortunes and was doing nothing to preserve or enlarge them. Outside was the scurry of Tientsin—Chinese voices, shrill and singsong, the rattle of trams, the honk of automobile horns. The only real thing was here in his hand.

Until now, Connor had not known just how much he depended on the old man down in the south—old Chang, his father's partner in all the great Connor interests that stretched half across China. Only Chang had known of his, Vincent Connor's, secret work; to Chang, he was no polo-playing dawdler, but a man who did things that changed the business and political life of all China. From Chang, too, had frequently come the call to action. But no more of those cryptic letters would arrive now.

Chang, on the inside of all the chaotic intrigue that had torn China asunder, was dead.

Connor stirred himself. He read the message again. Chang had been up the river at Changsha when the "red" army of General Ng Fu looted that city; he had been shot by General

"One false move—"
he warned.

Ng Fu, said the wire. Chang was a British subject, too, born in Hongkong. Lifting his eyes, Connor caught sight of the British vice-consul crossing the club lobby.

"I say, Foster!" he called, maintaining his casual mask with an effort. "Have you a moment? A question of diplomatic etiquette or something. Suppose one of your Hongkong subjects were to be killed by the Chinese—"

Foster groaned. "What redress, eh? None, my dear chap, none whatever, except a claim for damages against somebody. None of these bandit generals are responsible. We can't touch 'em, and as you know, there's no central government that can touch 'em. Like your Chicago gunmen. Best way is to wait until they kill each other off, ruin the country, and let some one man rise to the top of the stew."

"No punitive measures are possible, in such a case?"

"We've no Mussolini in England, old chap. More's the pity!"

Connor sank back into his chair and lit a cigarette, thoughtfully. True, China was in total chaos. There were plenty of patriotic Chinese, anxious for good government: men of affairs, educated men—but they were lost in a country gone mad with loot and graft. Men like old Chang.

"It's every man for himself," thought Connor. His sunburned features, wide-angled and resolute, set in grim lines. A sudden flash lighted the blue eyes under his black brows. "So! Then why not buy chips in the game, eh?"

The idea stirred in him. For months, now, he had worked beneath the surface, had handled job after job, for the sake of that China which had furnished his fortune and by which he now existed. None suspected his activity, though more than one European and Asiatic government wondered why its plans had gone amiss. But now—well, this was something different.

Connor stirred, took his hat and stick, and went down to the general offices where the Connor interests were handled. In his own office he caught up the telephone and finally ran Bert Swann to earth. Swann was not one of the socially elect. He had drifted in from somewhere with an airplane and a load of loot—rumor said that he had been flying for one of the war lords, and being unable to get any salary, had taken the crate and skipped with it. Probable enough, too.

"Swann? Connor speaking—Vincent Connor. Met you the other day at the races."

"Oh, sure! The gilded youth. I remember now," said Swann impolitely. "How's things?"

"Fair enough. Will that air wagon of yours fly?"

"Yeah, if the sheriff's after me it will. Why?"

"Come up to the Tientsin Club and lunch with me at one. We'll talk business."

"Can do. Thanks."

CONNOR'S GENERAL manager tapped and entered, an anxious look on his broad celestial face.

"A man is here, a Shensi man by his accent, though he can speak English. His name is Sui, but he says only that he wishes to see you privately. It is unusual, perhaps dangerous. He has the look of a rat."

Connor smiled. "The tiger does not fear rats. Let him enter."

Mr. Sui entered. He wore European clothes, and spoke perfect English. Accustomed from his boyhood to deal with Chinese, Connor read trickery and craft in the man's yellow face; a small man, with silky voice.

"You are Mr. Connor? I think I saw you at Yale, four years ago—you were graduating, and I was there for six months. I am sorry that I am not on a pleasant errand, Mr. Connor."

"Yes?" said Connor.

"You see, I represent General Ng Fu. You may have heard of him."

Connor nodded quietly. "Yes. He has gained some successes recently."

"He will gain more. He has now drawn back to Tienfu, to consolidate his conquests and reorganize his army," said Mr. Sui. "In the district which he now occupies, many of your business interests lie. There are mines, mills, and so forth. Not in your name, but owned by the companies you control."

Connor ground his cigarette in a tray, absently, and eyed the little man.

"You know a good deal about my affairs."

"I know all about them, for that is my business," said Mr. Sui complacently. "My master does not wish to disturb your commercial interests, but plans a complete industrial reorganization in his district. However, a contribution to his treasury—"

"I see, I see," and Connor smiled evenly. Either this agent knew nothing of Chang's murder, or attached no importance to it. "In plain words, blackmail and graft, eh? Well, that's the order of the day in China. What guarantee have I of your honesty?"

"I have a signed protection from General Ng Fu to give upon delivery of the money," said Sui eagerly. "This guarantees you as one of his friends and supporters. Immediately upon getting word from me, he issues protective orders to all of your business interests."

"I see." Connor looked thoughtfully at the other. "I should want to see you put your letter in the post, however—what is the sum demanded?"

"Fifty thousand dollars, gold."

"A hundred thousand Mex, eh? Do you accept checks?" asked Connor dryly.

"Of course."

"Very well," said Connor with the shrug of a man dismissing a boring piece of business. "I must do it, naturally. Hm! I'm playing polo this afternoon—dining with the Hardinges— suppose you come to the Tientsin Club at nine thirty to-night, eh? Bring your papers. How do you want the money?"

"In two checks, if you please." Sweat bedewed the yellow brow, for Mr. Sui had not anticipated so swift and easy a victory. "One for thirty thousand, one for twenty."

"Very well. At nine thirty. You'll be brought to my room at the club."

Mr. Sui departed, walking on air.

Bert Swann turned up at the appointed time, and Connor got a table for two in the corner of the club dining room. Swann was a Maine man, a drawling Yankee with a twang to his tongue, with a cold eye, a wide grin, and six feet of solid brawn.

"What do you want?" the flyer demanded bluntly. "Taxi service to Pekin?"

"No. To Tienfu," said Connor.

The other whistled softly. "Are you serious? That's inland and down south—"

"Listen, Swann—get me straight, now," and Connor met the cold eyes squarely. "I'm going to Tienfu. I want to be there before I'm expected. General Ng Fu is there, and I'm either going to shoot him or carry him off from the middle of his own army. Also, I'll have an unwilling passenger to take along. If possible, I want to leave early in the morning. There's part of the scheme on the table. What do you say?"

"Me? I say you're crazy, buddy. It just can't be done."

"Name your price. If we make a dicker, I'll let you in on the fun."

"And the firing squad, eh? All right." The cold eyes of Swann glimmered. "I guess maybe I figured you wrong, buddy. Are you hiring me or taking me in on the ground floor?"

"Suit yourself."

"All right. We're partners, and damn the money! Now give me the story."

AT NINE THIRTY that night, Connor was in his room at the club, with Bert Swann imbibing a long cold drink. Connor had given his general manager certain orders that day in regard to Mr. Sui, and knew they would be carried out to the letter.

When Sui arrived, sleek and debonair and inwardly excited, Connor introduced Swann, then seated himself at the table, opposite his yellow visitor. He produced the two checks demanded and laid them down, putting his Han jade paperweight upon them.

"I made these out to cash," Connor said amiably. "Now for your side of the pact."

Sui opened up his bulky brief case, got out Chinese writing materials and documents, and displayed a large and ornate document on red paper. It was a blank protection, signed by General Ng Fu; when Sui had filled in Connor's name, it told the world that Connor was the friend and supporter of Ng Fu and was to be treated as such.

Blandly pocketing the check for twenty thousand as his commission, Sui brushed a letter to the general inclosing the check for thirty thousand, as Connor's contribution, and giving the agreed terms—namely, that all the Connor enterprises in Ng Fu's district should be exempt from taxation or bother of any kind. He handed the letter to Connor, who, to his obvious surprise, read the characters aloud.

"Fair enough," said Connor. "I'll see that this is sent, myself, and will insure its delivery with the thirty thousand-dollar check to Ng Fu personally. Seal it. Then give me a receipt for the full fifty thousand, to go in my business records."

Sui sealed the letter and Ng Fu's check, which he was entirely willing to trust to Connor, and then wrote out the receipt demanded. The business was concluded. Buckling up his brief-case, he bowed to Connor and Swann, and then departed. Swann grinned.

"And he fell for it! Say, buddy, I got to hand it to you."

"You'd better go pound your ear," suggested Connor, "if we're to leave at six in the morning. Rain, fog, or whirlwind, we've got to go."

"We will," said Swann. "We'll have gas enough to make Tienfu, but we'll need a whole lot of luck. This is a crazy party all the way!"

"It'll have a sane ending," said Connor grimly. Chang had been more than a right-hand man to him. He had been like a benevolent old uncle; and his face loomed before Connor's eyes.

Ten minutes later his general manager called up to say that instructions had been followed. Mr. Sui had been collared on leaving the club, and was in safe keeping.

Six in the morning saw Swann warming up his machine—a Class A monoplane with Whirlwind engine and a gun mounted forward. Connor arrived in his Sunbeam, and the two men with him jerked a frightened, wailing bundle out of the car and into the cabin of the plane.

"Our friend Sui, all complete, even to the brief-case," Connor told the aviator. "Ready? Let's go."

"High time," said Swann. "Some damned government has served notice on me that I can't leave. I dunno how they expect to keep me—"

The rest was lost in the roar of the engine.

So they circled in the sunrise, above the lazy Taku river and its shipping, and over the town and foreign concessions, and straight for the hills. After all, it was far from being so crazy as it seemed or sounded, for Sui's briefcase had yielded a recent map of Tienfu with everything pricked out in detail, including the air field General Ng Fu had constructed for his budding aerial force. And there was only a bit over five hundred miles to go, bee line.

Mr. Sui protested volubly, but nobody paid any attention to him, and he was so securely tied that he could be safely neglected.

"You've been up before?" said Bert Swann, eying this secretive partner of his curiously.

Connor smiled. "I got my pilot's license in my last year at college—that was some time ago, though. Yes, I've been up a few times since. This is a good crate."

"Fairish," admitted Swann, and plunged into a discussion of air-fighting in China.

Connor had brought a basket of lunch, little of which was wasted on the captive, though he was not allowed to suffer. Bert Swann had no map, but flew by compass alone; yet now and again he pointed out objects below—mountains, towns, rivers. Connor marveled.

"It's my job," said the flyer. "I made it my business to know China from the air. No good maps. I can fly anywhere by compass—that is, in the north. I don't know the south so well, down around Yunnan and Canton, and I haven't touched the west. But I've pulled some queer stunts around these parts!"

"You're a wonder," said Connor. The other gave him a queer look.

"So are you, for that matter. I've heard a lot about you— society bird and so on. Nobody thinks you're worth a damn, any more than the average rich youth."

"And what do you think?" queried Connor.

"Quit kidding me, buddy." Swann grinned. "We'll get on, you and I."

THE MILES sped behind, with never a miss in the motor; hour after hour sped away, while the stiff and miserable Sui begged unavailingly for mercy and freedom. Finally Swann pointed to a range of low hills a short distance ahead.

"There y'are. Beyond them, we'll pick up the river. Tienfu should be about thirty miles south—we're on the big bend here, you know. Ng Fu has two old Jennies, bombers. Might sell him this crate."

Connor nodded. "That's what I intend—only you'll never get any money for it."

Swann laughed gayly, and shot him an admiring glance.

"All right—you're the doctor!"

"Got any ammunition for that gun?" said Connor. "If you have, get it ready as soon as we land. Then trail along with me and see what turns up."

The other nodded.

The hills fled below and behind and they pick up the silver ribbon of the river. Swann came down to two thousand feet, glanced again at Sui's map of the city, and presently Tienfu drew into sight. The landing field, and General Ng Fu's headquarters as well, were outside the old walled town.

Presently they were over the camp and field, and their arrival created obvious excitement, until it was seen that they were descending peacefully. Connor's eyes kindled as he stared down. He knew well that he was doing an absolutely crazy thing, from all normal viewpoints, yet he was thoroughly enjoying himself.

"Good discipline," and he nodded toward the field below, which had been cleared as by magic. "Forming up in ranks— hm!"

The crowd about two airplanes had melted. The rows of tents showed precision; hospital, headquarters, ammunition and food dumps—the whole place had a very military look, by no means usual with China's bandit armies. The machine swooped, landed perfectly, and taxied to a halt before the two Jennies and their hangars.

There was no outrush of the crowd. Two officers, alone, came striding out to the plane, as Connor clambered out. One of the two stepped forward and saluted him briskly.

"I am Colonel Wang Lin, of General Ng Fu's staff," he said in English.

Connor smiled, gave his name, and then proceeded in Mandarin of the old florid style:

"Present the compliments of this unworthy slave to the great venerable ancestor, before whom the earth trembles! I have brought with me one Sui, the Tientsin agent of the lordly maternal uncle, and certain sums of money. I desire an audience—"

"Refreshment awaits you, elder cousin," returned the officer. "Also an audience. Pray come with me, and my men will refuel and condition your machine. Will your pilot accompany us?"

Connor assented, and Bert Swann, leaving helmet and leather coat, fell in with them, slamming the cabin door. Mr. Sui was left to his lamentations.

They proceeded toward headquarters—an old temple a quarter mile distant whose surrounding grove of trees had not been disturbed. Connor knew that he would have no difficulty in seeing his man. The average war lord, upon attaining power, became more invisible than the Son of Heaven, and was invariably surrounded by purchasing agents, grafters, and guards; but Ng Fu had not attained such heights, and was said to be almost democratic in his sway.

Ten minutes later, in fact, they were in his presence.

A room of the temple had been cleared, whitewashed, laid with mats. By the unglazed window was a table littered with maps and papers; behind this sat the bandit general—a man of about fifty, with heavy-lidded eyes behind thick spectacles, lines of humor about his mouth, a firm and resolute countenance. Connor would have liked him at first glance, if it had not been for—Chang.

Upon learning the identity of his visitor, Ng Fu shook hands, ordered in tea and cakes and cigarettes, and abandoned all formality.

"I have heard of you," he said in fluent Mandarin, for he was a man of education. "And you have come all this way to see me? When did you leave Tientsin? That is marvelous! What is this about my agent, the traitorous Sui?"

Connor told him, while the listening officers stared silently.

"Here is the sealed letter addressed to you, general. Have the man searched, and you will find the other check in his pocket, I presume. Here is the receipt—"

"For fifty thousand dollars," said Ng Fu, and tore open the sealed letter. He produced the check for thirty thousand. A few words to one of his officers, who left the room, and he smiled grimly at Connor. "We shall see."

Refreshments were brought in. Presently the officer returned and laid the check for twenty thousand dollars before the general, who nodded and turned to Connor.

"You did well to bring that grafting rascal to me! Your story is true. I should like to buy this airplane in which you came; it is far better than my machines. What is your price?"

Connor turned to Bert Swann, who, understood little or no Mandarin, and put the question.

"The sky's the limit, buddy," and Swann grinned. "Twenty thousand, or I'll take five."

"Twenty thousand dollars, general," Connor translated, conscious that more than one of the officers around probably understood English. "I think it is too much—"

"Not a cent too much," said Ng Fu cordially. "Here is the money." And he handed Connor the check for twenty thousand. "Now that it is all settled—"

There was a ragged discharge of rifles outside. Connor started, bewildered as he was by the crafty financial manipulation of the bandit general. The latter waved his hand amiably.

"That is nothing—only the execution of my late Tientsin

agent. I am anxious to talk with you about the military situation. Here, look at this map—"

HALF AN hour later, the general beamed upon his visitor. "Tell me, were you not afraid to venture thus into my hands? Did it not occur to you that I might hold you to ransom or kill you?"

Connor shrugged. Bert Swann, tiring of the talk, had gone forth to look after his machine and gun, and search for something solid in the way of food.

"I didn't think of that, particularly," Connor returned casually. "Would you like to inspect this airplane? It is a fighting machine, and has some interesting features."

"By all means," returned the general heartily. "One moment, until I give certain orders—we are expecting an attack at any time, you know. Have a fresh cigarette."

Connor nodded, and glanced over the map on the desk, while Ng Fu gave orders in regard to certain ammunition and supplies, now being camouflaged.

As Connor now understood, the bandit general was in a bad way. In retiring from Changsha he had broken with the main communist forces, and his district was now hemmed in by the Nationalist armies, who might be encamped around him for weeks or months, after the fashion of Chinese warfare. While Ng Fu was solidly organized, he could not remain inactive forever, and was facing hugely superior forces. His one hope was that diversions from other quarters might draw the Nationalist armies off and give him a weak point at which to strike. The enemy had a number of airplanes, whose bombs had already damaged him sadly, but he had gone in for camouflage. A shrewd fellow, Ng Fu, ahead of his comrade war lords in brains and craft.

"All ready?"

Attended by four staff officers Connor and the general walked out together, and strode over to the hangers. Again Connor was struck by the discipline prevailing; and Ng Fu pointed out that none of his men were allowed in the town, strict order being kept.

"My district is not a conquered province," he said, "but a source of revenue from well-governed people."

Connor thought of old Chang, shot down without mercy, and his lips tightened.

Coming to the field, Connor saw that Swann was at the controls, warming up his engine, which was allowed to idle as they approached. The mechanics had finished their work. With Connor beside him and the four officers following, General Ng Fu strode toward the machine, beside whose cockpit a set of steps had been placed. Just outside the rush of air from the propeller, he halted, while Connor pointed out the construction and lines of the plane. As he did so, he caught the eye of Swann and gestured slightly. The pilot donned his goggles.

Then, abruptly, Connor slipped the automatic pistol from his armpit holster and jammed it against the neck of the general.

"Tell your officers to fall back!" he exclaimed sharply. "Quick, now! One false move from you or them, and you're done for! March up those steps."

Sharp cries of dismay arose. Connor reached around his prisoner and secured Ng Fu's pistol. Shouts began to go up from every hand, as the plight of their leader was revealed; a babel of discord arose from the watching ranks. Yet it was so obvious that the general himself would catch the first reprisal, that not a shot was fired. Before the astounded, disconcerted watchers could quite realize what was happening, Connor was marching his prisoner up the steps and into the cabin of the machine. Then he slammed the door, which was self-locking.

Swann, at the forward controls, gave her the gun instantly and the engine screamed. Thirty seconds later she was off the ground. Swann turned and grinned.

"Where to, buddy?"

Connor pointed straight up.

"Get altitude and then make for Changsha."

"Got you."

The impossible had been accomplished.

GENERAL NG FU sat holding on very tightly to his chair; never before had he been in the air, but his stolid, impassive countenance betrayed no emotion. Swann climbed steadily into a blue sky speckled with clouds. Presently Ng Fu had the unique experience of looking down upon a foamy white sea of cloud and seeing the plane's shadow there.

"Bert!" Connor lifted his voice. "Cut the gun when you get high enough. Want to talk."

Connor hitched his seat around. Ng Fu looked at the pistol, then met Connor's gaze, his sloe-black eyes hard as black jade. All of a sudden there was comparative silence, as the engine was cut down to idling.

"Ng Fu, I'm taking you to Changsha," said Connor. "And I want you to know why."

"I can guess," said the other stolidly. "How much are they paying you? I will double it."

Connor laughed harshly, disagreeably.

"You will not," he retorted. "When your army sacked Changsha, you shot a man deliberately. That man was my friend and partner, Chang Ti-shan, a man known over half of China—a good and wise man, venerated by all who knew him. Because of that act, I'm going to turn you over to the Nationalists and you can stand before a firing squad."

A startled expression leaped into the black eyes.

"What? Is this—do you believe this?"

"I received word of it yesterday. Chang was shot three day's ago."

General Ng Fu regarded him steadily for a moment, then slowly smiled.

"What you say of Chang Ti-shan is true," he rejoined. "He was my friend also; he is what Confucius called a superior man."

"And you had him shot, you devil!" said Connor.

"On the contrary. My army did not sack Changsha—that was done by the communists. I kept my troops out of the city. Word came to me that Chang Ti-shan had been seized by the communist chiefs and was to be shot. I went with my bodyguard to their headquarters and took him away in safety. That is why the armies split asunder. The Russian agents with the communist forces were very, very angry. They are not superior men, I have decided."

Connor felt as though the clouds were splitting to let him drop through.

"What?" he cried. In those impassive black eyes he read the truth. "You—can you prove this, Ng Fu?"

"Chang is down there in Tienfu at this moment. I have appointed him governor of the city."

"Good Lord!" Connor sank back, let the pistol fall. "But you must have known about the report—"

"It was good. If China thought that Chang Ti-shan had been shot, it would provoke a wave of resentment. I have found that the communists are selfish men, poor soldiers, dupes of Russian agents." Ng Fu shrugged a little. "So we decided to let the report go out."

Connor stared at his prisoner in dismay. Then, if this were true—

"Hey, buddy!" Bert Swann turned, his voice urgent. "Lock those two steel bars and do it quick! Fasten the belts—move, durn you, move! There's three crates in that cloud ahead—"

"Go on back to Tienfu," ordered Connor.

"You durn fool, jump! You'll be in Hades first thing you know!"

Connor woke up.

Two steel bars locked the chairs in position. He caught the general's safety belt and hurriedly snapped it, then his own; and just in time. The engine sputtered and roared into life.

Bullets smashed into the safety-glass of the window beside

them. The three planes were from the Nationalist forces, and took the monoplane for one of Ng Fu's crates.

WHAT FOLLOWED was, momentarily, a wild chaos.

Bert Swann went into a dive, with tracer bullets smoking around him—the three had caught him at a bad moment, and were out to get him. They were old DH machines, however, no match for his fast fighter, once he got into action—and Swann lost no time getting into action.

The chairs swayed dizzily, but were held fast. Out of the dive into a sharp turn, a swift upward zoom; the Hotchkiss gun burst into a quick rattle. A side-slip—

Connor now saw one of the DH machines fluttering down like a bird with a broken wing. The impassive Chinese flinched suddenly—the glass beside him leaped full of holes. Blood spurted from his arm. He made no sound, sat stolidly as ever, after that first startled jump.

Then a wild swoop, a sharp sidewise turn—directly before them showed a second DH, and Swann opened up viciously. The other machine went to pieces in mid-air. Up shot Swann, up and around; the third enemy had taken warning, however, and had straightened out in desperate, frantic flight.

"Hey, buddy!" Swann turned tensed, excited features. "I can get him—"

"No—back down!" ordered Connor.

Swann obeyed.

When General Ng Fu, one bandaged arm in an improvised sling, stepped out onto solid earth again, he was greeted by a storm of cheers and wild yells; and with reason. He was the only one of China's war lord bandits who could boast of actual air-fighting, and had a scar to show for it. And Connor, leaving the plane, saw a thin old figure in black silk garments among a crowd of officers—Chang the venerable!

Half an hour later, Connor and Swann sat once more in headquarters, with the general and old Chang, sipping their tea.

Ng Fu had just torn up Connor's checks totaling fifty thousand dollars. When the general finished speaking, Connor turned with a grin to the aviator.

"Bert! He says you're offered a colonel's commission, five hundred gold a month, and the command of his air force. What say?"

"Done," said Swann delightedly.

"I'm to be his Tientsin agent—and he wants three more planes like yours. Also, he's buying yours. Five thousand cash. Suit you?"

"You bet."

Connor turned again to the general.

"He agrees, but must take me back to Tientsin in the morning, after his engine is overhauled. I'll go to work at once—you must avoid any further conflict with the Nationalists until I can get into touch with them. We'll throw you into their party."

Ng Fu chuckled.

"Yes, I think so myself," he rejoined. "Chiang Kai-shek cannot be beaten as a general. Nor can I match forces with him. But, allied with you and him and Chang Ti-shan, there is a chance—"

"For all of us," and old Chang's wrinkled features broke into a smile.

Connor wondered what they would say at the Tientsin Club—if they knew! But they never would.

V

CONNOR TAKES CHARGE

To manage a Far East business in spite of Chinese intrigues takes both courage and brains; and Vincent Connor's friends never guessed he had either.

CHAPTER I

EMPIRE BUILDERS

CONNOR WAS well aware of the rather oblique directions in which news travels, particularly in China; a thousand miles away from a given point, one may know better what is going on than persons there. He was not surprised, therefore, when the blow fell.

He was lunching, after a morning's work-out at polo, with a light-headed, giddy young British *attaché* just down from Mukden, full of Manchurian news and anxious to show off how much he knew. To him, as to every one else in Tientsin, Connor was a pleasant but negligible fellow who had inherited vast commercial interests in China, enjoyed life, and was not to be taken seriously.

"I say, aren't there Connor interests down in Yunnan?" he asked abruptly.

"Rather!" Connor chuckled. "Tin mine at Muling, various things in Yunnan City, and so on. Why?"

"Better sell out," said the other, wagging his head sagely. "Can't say anything, you know; but the jolly old province is in for a hot time. Mark my words, some of these days we'll wake up to see it grabbed by the frog-eaters."

"So?" queried Connor, his eyes narrowing slightly. "If France did seize Yunnan, your tight little isle would let out a wild roar, and the rooster would drop the corncob."

"Never heard of a corncob," said the other. "London's in a bad way; coalition government and what not. Deuced bad way!

Can't let out any roars. Besides, who knows? Tit for tat, and all that sort of thing. Sell out your Yunnan interests, old chap."

Three drinks later, Connor returned cautiously to the subject, and his guest thawed a bit. A deft query pried loose a pearl of information.

"You'll see a devilish clever chappie bob up in the south one day. He was in Mukden a fortnight ago. A remarkable fellow and all that, name of Wang Yin. Oxford and Sorbonne; been in Russia a year or so."

At this instant the British consul sauntered over to their table, and Connor's source of information was immediately frozen.

Although he had two horses entered in the afternoon racing, Connor chucked the events, turned over his box to friends, and drove back to the city. He did not go to his office, but direct to the Tientsin Club, where he dispatched several telegrams, and after calling various numbers, at length tracked down the man he wanted—Severn, the Australian distance flyer, who had landed three days previously in the Taku River after a flight

*The Chinese
fell limp.*

from Seattle to Japan, and who was bound for Australia. He spoke rapidly, and Severn assented.

"I'll be over in twenty minutes, Connor. Come to your room? Right."

Connor hung up, lit a cigarette, and stared at the map on his room wall.

MORE THAN mere money was at stake now, and he realized it with startled alarm. Connor was one of the many white men in China who sincerely admired the old nation, who had been fighting to save it from anarchy and worse, and who saw themselves slowly defeated by greed and selfish ambition. No one knew or dreamed of Connor's interest, however, except two or three Chinese who could be trusted.

"Mm! This Wang Yin was in Mukden; some sort of a deal was made with the British," he reflected, and gazed at the map thoughtfully.

North and South China were as usual at handgrips. Manchuria, where one or two alleged Japanese spies had just been shot, was under the threat of seizure by Japan. Yunnan, off to the south and with French influence predominant and upholding its grim old governor in power, enjoyed peace; though war was just across its borders. Indo-China was seething with revolt against the French, while Burma had just been in open rebellion against Britain.

And England herself was in the throes of financial and political crisis—an emergency which, some said, meant the end of the Crimson Empire. No, the British Lion was in no position to roar if the French seized Yunnan and added it to their colonial empire. Already they held it in a tight commercial grip.

A telegram arrived, a tremendously long telegram. It was in Chinese, and it was also in code. The signature told Connor that it had come from old Chang, who had been his father's partner, and who, from his retirement in Shanghai, kept in close touch with all the affairs of China. He settled down to decode it, for Connor spoke and wrote Chinese more fluently than the majority of the yellow race themselves; it was a long task, however, and he was still working at it when Severn arrived— a tall, rangy, sandy-haired man of thirty.

Connor set out cigarettes and a drink, and settled down.

"Severn, I want to get down to Yunnan City," he said abruptly. "In a straight line, it's about a thousand miles. By way of the coast, it's an impossibility; I want to get there as quickly as possible, a non-stop flight. There's a good landing field at Cheng-tu, about halfway, if you have to make a stop."

"A thousand miles?" said Severn cheerfully. "Can do—rather, could do if necessary, old chap. I'd like to oblige, but I've made my plans to go by way of Shanghai and Hongkong, and then down to Saigon—"

"Change them," broke in Connor, and pushed across the table a check he had previously filled out. The airman glanced at it, picked it up and inspected it a second time, and looked up amazedly at his host.

"Can do?" asked Connor dryly. "It would mean leaving here

in the morning, and keeping my identity secret. I don't want a soul to know that I'm going. When I get there, I'll leave you immediately. You can make up your own yarn to account for it."

"To-morrow morning before daylight, eh?" Severn squinted down at the check, then glanced at his watch. He folded the check across, slowly, then thrust it into his pocket and reached for his drink. "Can do. How!"

TEN MINUTES later Connor, alone once more, resumed his work on the telegram. A slow whistle broke from him as he realized its import, but not until he had finished the last phrase did he pick up the translated sheet and give it his full attention. Then he realized how shrewdly he had acted in making his deal with Severn at the first possible moment. The message made clear to him an appalling situation:

> Total disaster threatens house of Han. No action possible as storm will break within week. Our friends in Yunnanfu are dead. Only Sung remains, hiding at Hei Lung. Communications dead. Person about whom you inquire undoubtedly agent for French interests planning extensive outbreak. Governor Yuan will ascend dragon, but blind and deaf. Am helpless.

Connor translated this still further in his own mind, as he read it over. Governor Yuan, war-lord of Yunnan, was an able and honest ruler; he was doomed to death and would listen to no warnings. Wang Yin was the center of everything; he probably planned some revolutionary outbreak designed to give the French a pretext to move in. Those with whom old Chang were in touch down there had been wiped out, and the one remaining person, Sung, was hiding. Hei Lung undoubtedly meant the Hei Lung or Black Dragon temple, a famous place just outside of Yunnan City. The plot would burst in a week's time or less, and from it would come the ruin of all China.

"So there's the game—as much of it as Chang can tell me, at least!" thought Connor, laying down the paper. "A thousand miles; well, Severn could make it by to-morrow night, for that Albatross of his is a devil for speed, and if not forced down he could manage it easily. There's a good landing field at Yunnan, too. All right. Get there, look up this chap Sung, and go to work. And now for camouflage!"

He called up his office, arranged for cashier's checks in a large amount to be sent over to him, checks good at the Banque Industrielle branch in Yunnan, and then packed his belongings for the trip.

At four o'clock he reached the Jockey Club, sauntered into his own box, and was warmly congratulated. His horse had won the Peking Plate twenty minutes before. Connor fell into light-hearted chatter with his friends. He was leaving in the morning for Peiping to get hold of some antique bronzes recently brought to light there, he said; and knowing grins went around.

"Poor Connor!" observed one lady, sotto voce, to a visitor from Hongkong. "A charming fellow, but he has no sense of business at all. He says he just buys anything that is thrown at him—does not know what to do with his money!"

CHAPTER II

A TEMPLE CONFERENCE

AT TEN thirty the next night Connor secured a room at the Terminus Hotel, in Yunnan City.

All the excitement and publicity centered about Severn, who had landed unheralded and unexpected. His passenger had no difficulty in slipping away with his bag and getting a car into the city, and as his papers were quite in order, he aroused only a superficial curiosity. No one here knew Connor personally. The wealthy idler and sportsman of Tientsin, whose father had built up a huge industrial heritage for him, was here only another foreign devil, and his name aroused no comment what-ever.

After a good night's sleep Connor breakfasted and sought out the hotel manager, a polite Frenchman. He was quite the tourist, with a camera slung over his shoulder, and explained that he wanted to take pictures of the Black Dragon Temple. This was entirely natural, and the manager arranged to have a guide and horses around in twenty minutes, at a price, the temple being ten miles northeast of the city.

"Any danger from bandits?" asked Connor timorously.

The Frenchman chuckled. "*M'sieu*, Yunnan has no bandits! You are safe, absolutely safe."

Connor nodded and strolled out, delighted with the beauty of the city, which lay on the east side of a lake above twenty miles long, with girdling hills and mountain peaks closing the horizon. He realized that this was the practically independent capital of a huge province, with its own telegraphs, telephone and electric system, mint and arsenal, as he strolled about, finding soldiers everywhere—brown, alert, smiling men. The friendliness and hospitality of Yunnan were proverbial.

"Damned shame!" thought Connor as he returned to the hotel, to find a guide awaiting him with horses. "To ruin all this in order to let France grab off a new colonial empire! But it isn't done yet."

Connor admitted to no knowledge of Chinese, but the native guide spoke French, so all was well. They mounted and set off at a brisk pace.

Thus, an hour later they were approaching the temple in its mountain grove of towering trees. The temple guarded the famous Black Dragon spring, which gushed from the limestone and carried fertility to the plain below—clear, cold mountain water. As they dismounted before the inclosed terrace, Connor saw a monk standing in the sunlight watching them.

He turned to the guide. "Remain here. I wish to take pictures and see the place by myself."

"But, *m'soo!*" protested the native volubly. "One must inter- pret—"

"One must obey," said Connor, his tone checking further argument. "You will be well paid none the less. I may stop here for lunch. Your business is to remain with the horses."

Leaving the astonished guide staring after him, he turned to the terrace and the entrance, where the impassive monk eyed him. Going up to the man, Connor addressed him.

"Venerable ancestor, I am named Connor. I have come from Tientsin at the bidding of one who is named Chang, I desire to see a man named Sung."

"I will see if there is any such person here," returned the priest. "Follow."

Connor was led into one of the side rooms of the central hall and bidden to wait. In five minutes he saw before him a man wearing the robes of a priest, but without the three holes burned in his shaven head that mark a Buddhist monk. The face was wrinkled, shrewd, kindly.

"Is this a miracle performed by Kwanyin?" said Sung, regarding Connor.

"No," and Connor smiled a little. "The venerable Chang told me you were here. I came. It is possible that we may do something, but I must have information from you."

"I am a relative by marriage of the honorable Chang," said the other calmly. "Let us sit down. My friends and those who managed your interests here are dead. I am alone, sought far and wide. They knew we would imperil their plans, you see. I dare not leave this roof, or be seen by any one. I can give you no help."

Connor sank into a great temple-chair of carved wood.

"Information is help," he said, seeing that the man before him was despondent and hopeless. "Tell me where to find Wang Yin, what he is like, and his plans."

"You know much already!" exclaimed Sung, starting slightly at mention of Wang's name.

Connor nodded calmly. "That is why I am here."

"You can do nothing."

"That is not for you to judge. Tell me what I seek, or I will go elsewhere."

"I WILL tell you; why such haste?" said Sung, and sat on a stool of porcelain. "Wang Yin is very clever, far too clever for these French agents with whom he deals. They think that he is going to break out in a revolt, destroy foreign property, probably kill a few white people, seize the palace and kill the governor. He will set himself up as ruler, and then the French will move up their troops by the railroad, capture Wang, and retire him on a pension. That is their program. They will then rule Yunnan, as they rule Annam and Tonkin."

Connor whistled softly. "I see! But Wang is too smart for them—how?"

"He has made his plans better than they know. He will seize the palace and kill the governor, yes; old Yuan means well and is honest, but refuses to listen to stories of plots. Then, instead of destroying foreign property, Wang Yin will protect it, will kill no white people."

"Oh! He'll double-cross the French, after he gets what he wants?"

"Exactly," and Sung nodded. "Instead of revolution, widespread destruction, fire, there will be only a short, savage capture of the palace. Wang will be giving orders instead of Yuan. The army will obey him, for the army obeys the paymaster. He has an administrative government ready to function immediately, even his proclamations are printed and ready for distribution."

"I see," said Connor. "Then, how will China be disrupted by his success?"

"Because Wang Yin is a communist," said Sung. "His chief men and aides here, like himself, have been trained in Russia, are backed by Russian support. Once he is in power, he is joined by the Cantonese Reds. He makes Yunnan a communistic state, threatening Burma on one flank, Indo-China on another. French and British will join hands to crush him. The most orderly and prosperous province of China will be devastated by communism, by war, by all manner of chaos, even as the north now is. Even without war, Wang Yin will institute communism here, and the result will be the same. Better to continue as we are."

"Infinitely, of course," said Connor. "When does Wang's coup take place?"

"Within the next three days."

"Shorter and shorter, eh? H'm! Is Wang himself here in Yunnanfu?"

"Yes. He uses his own name. He has rented the Evremond villa, near the lake, and is living there with certain of his aides. No women. But why do you ask? You are helpless."

Connor dropped his cigarette, leaned back in his chair.

"Venerable Sung," he said dryly, "for the past ninety years, ever since the Opium War, foreign diplomats have visualized just one way of grabbing portions of China—by intervention following the murder of missionaries or other foreign devils. It has worked like a charm, and no new process has ever been necessary. Within the past year, I myself have broken up two or three identical attempts, working along the same old lines. The innocent bystander is the main sufferer, and some foreign interest or country is the gainer. Now, my venerable friend, it does not pay to try to beat such a man as Wang Yin at his own game."

"It does not," agreed Sung mournfully. "My son was one of his aides; he is dead. My family and friends are dead. We thought that we were clever."

Connor rose. "I am not clever," he said crisply. "At all events, not clever enough to match wits with Wang Yin and on his own ground."

"Then you realize that you can do nothing?"

"Eh?" Connor smiled slightly. "Not at all. I can try to do everything, and I shall. With the proper break of luck, I may pull some of your chestnuts out of the fire. Tell me whether there is one man in Yunnan City on whom I can rely for information, help, advice. One man who will obey me and ask no questions."

Sung's wrinkled features were anxious, as he peered at Connor.

"There is one such man, yes," he said slowly. "No one knows that he was associated with me; much of our information came from him. His name is Tsing Fan, and he is a porter at the Hotel Terminus."

"Eh? A porter!" exclaimed Connor.

The other smiled slightly.

"The peacock pretends to be a sparrow, that no one may steal his feathers." Sung removed a large Buddhist rosary from about his neck and extended it. "Give him this, and he will know that you are the man. I can do no more for you."

"That is enough," said Connor, and rose.

Outside, he rejoined his guide, said curtly that he was not staying for lunch after all, and headed back for the city.

It was past noon when they reached the hotel. Connor lunched there, then spoke with the manager, asking to have the porter Tsing Fan sent to his room.

"A friend who was here recently recommended him to me," he said negligently, "and he may be of service."

"At once, *m'sieu*," was the response, and Connor went on to his room.

CONNOR LOOKED curiously at the man who entered. Tsing Fan was apparently young, very stalwart, his face keenly intelligent; but, in the hotel uniform and cap, he looked like a fish out of water. Tsing Fan closed the door, and spoke in French.

"You sent for me, *m'sieu?*"

"This unworthy little brother requested the honor of your presence," said Connor in the most formal Mandarin. The other started slightly; his eyes became alert, suspicious. "You are acquainted with the venerable Sung, I believe?"

"There is no such family, to my knowledge," said Tsing Fan. Connor laughed and pointed to the bed.

"Lift up the pillow."

Tsing Fan hesitated, then went to the bed and lifted the pillow. He saw the big rosary lying there, dropped the pillow, turned with a sharp exclamation.

"What!"

"Sit down and talk," said Connor. "I have come from Tientsin at the request of my old friend and partner, Chang. I have seen Sung. He says that you will obey me."

"That is so, heaven-born," murmured Tsing Fan, staring at him. "Connor! I know now. You are of that family in the north."

"Exactly," said Connor. "Will you help me against Wang Yin, or not?"

"This humble slave is at your command, venerable ancestor," murmured the other, dazedly. He sat down. "You have but to ask."

"You know the Evremond Villa where the man Wang lives?"

Tsing Fan looked up, and his eyes flashed.

"Yes. It is within, large grounds, above the lake."

"Guarded?"

"Men watch the grounds, yes. The servants came with Wang Yin, and are his men."

"How many?"

"Two or three. I cannot say certainly."

"The villa has a telephone?"

"Yes."

Connor regarded the man intently. "When one treads upon the tiger's tail," he said in the familiar locution, "it is necessary to step swiftly. Wang Yin is undoubtedly on his guard against any sort of attack. He is too clever to be met with guile. Am I right?"

Tsing Fan assented. "He watches the foreign colony closely.

By this time he must know of your arrival. I myself heard you came with Severn."

"Are you willing to go with me to-night to his villa?"

"Of course!" The dark, oblique eyes flashed again. "What will you do there?"

"I do not know," said Connor frankly. "It depends on what turns up when I talk with him. His men are armed?"

Tsing Fan laughed bitterly. "Have not our friends and relatives been killed like flies in the past two weeks? They are killers, all of them. I have talked with merchants who went to that villa. They say every one who comes is searched for arms."

Connor's eyes narrowed. "So? Valuable news. Have you other clothes than those you wear now?"

"I have nothing, excellency," said the other. "I am a house-boy, a pewter. I play the part. I live up under the eaves with two others in the same room. Thus, I have never been suspected of being other than I seem."

"Very well," said Connor. "Have you a knife?"

"Yes."

"Bring it. Be here at eight o'clock to-night."

"Very well," said Tsing Fan composedly. "You bear the rosary of Sung; therefore you are to be obeyed in all things. But I tell you that we cannot enter that villa unseen. We could not get past the gates."

"We shall not enter unseen," and Connor smiled. "There are plenty of rent-cars here? Pick the best automobile you can find, hire it for an hour, and have it here at eight. That is all. Here is money."

Tsing Fan departed. Connor sallied forth, engaged a guide at the hotel entrance, and set out for the bazaars. There, through the guide, he purchased an outfit of the finest Soochow silk, such as a wealthy Chinese gentleman might wear; he was outrageously cheated, but he dared not let any one guess that he spoke the language himself. A coolie was engaged to carry the parcels, lest the guide lose face, and so Connor came back to the hotel, with the afternoon largely spent.

HE REMAINED in his room until dinner time, then descended and dined in leisurely manner, and learned that Severn had taken off successfully that morning to continue his flight to Saigon. Returning to his room, he took a brief-case from his bag, emptied out the papers it contained, and in their place put a slender whalebone slung shot. A knock sounded at his door. It was precisely eight o'clock as Tsing Fan entered.

Connor pointed to the outfit on the bed.

"Get into them. Where's your knife?"

He whistled softly as Tsing Fan produced a wickedly curved blade, thin and razor-edged. Connor tucked it into the brief-case and buckled the latter shut. Then, taking one of his own engraved cards, he went to the writing desk and sat down. Beneath his name he wrote in English:

> Bringing letters from Mukden. Also Yao Erh Sze of Canton. Urgent. Confidential.

Pocketing the card, he rose and surveyed Tsing Fan, who grinned widely in his new outfit, and looked vastly different. Connor dived into his bag and produced his make-up box.

"You need a few marks of age, my friend, and a mustache. I can provide them in a few moments." As he provided them, he went on talking. "I have been thinking just what I should do, were I in Wang Yin's place and occupying that villa, and receiving callers.

"Now, here are your orders! You are to say and do nothing, except to say that you are a friend of mine and bear certain proposals from the Canton government, supplementing my own proposals. Don't say this unless forced. Your all-important task is to watch me. After I have opened this brief-case, be ready. When I put my hand inside it—switch off the lights. Then seize your knife from inside the case and if anybody comes into the room—get him. Is that quite clear?"

"Very well," said Tsing Fan, with a nod. "Suppose your mind is changed after you get there?"

"Then I'll give you a shake of the head—no!" exclaimed Connor. "In that case, I'll not open the brief case at all, which is better still. But time yourself carefully, and don't jump for the electric switch until my hand slides into the case. There's your mustache. Take a look at yourself and let's go. If the hotel people wonder who the strange Chinaman is, no matter. The car is waiting? Tell the driver to go to some tea-house here. Once we're away from the hotel, direct him to the villa."

Together they descended the stairs and passed out of the hotel. A battered Mercedes was waiting in front, with a French driver. Tsing Fan gave him an address, and changed it a moment later, once they were off.

Connor could not but admire the blind and implicit manner in which Tsing Fan had obeyed him, without asking explanations, without protests. Knowing that their driver could neither hear nor understand, he touched the other's knee and spoke quietly in Mandarin.

"You are thinking that it is strange I have not told you what I mean to do?" He felt Tsing Fan start at these words, and laughed softly. "My friend, it is simply that I do not know. I gamble everything on what turns up at the moment. We may go to disaster; certainly we go to danger; but what we do is not for ourselves."

"Thank you," said Tsing Fan. "It is for the millions of people around us; I quite understand, my friend."

In his tone was a certain dignity which impressed Connor, as they relied along.

SOON THEY were out of the brilliantly lighted streets, passing through tree-shaded avenues of the residential quarter built up by the foreign element; the walls, high hedges, stout gates, bespoke French influence. The car turned in before two high iron gates, blocked to a height of six feet with plates of sheet-iron, and the driver honked insistently. The gates were opened enough to give exit to a native, who barked a question. Connor leaned from the window and beckoned, holding out his card.

"Take this to your master," he said, "and admit us promptly."

Within the grounds showed the lights of a house. The man took the card and passed it to another inside the gates. The French driver talked to himself, with frequent curses on the insolence of the yellow race. After a moment a bell jingled and the native threw open the gates, gesturing them to pass on.

"Am I to wait, *messieurs?*" asked the driver.

"No. This is all we require," said, Contser. "We shall walk back—perhaps."

They drew up beneath a *porte-cochère;* this villa, it appeared, was a pretentious place, at least on the outside, though it did not seem a large building. A light flashed out overhead, and a black-clad Chinese appeared and bowed slightly.

"My master will receive you at once, gentlemen," he said in perfect French. "Follow me, if you please. Do you wish to see him in company, or separately?"

Connor had anticipated this query, which indicated success. Two callers would be received with more suspicion than one, unless their business was plausible.

"We have letters to present that mention us both, in regard to certain matters," he responded. "When these have been attended to, my business with him is confidential—as, I believe, is that of M. Yao, here."

"He will be at liberty in a moment, and requests that you wait here," and the servant showed them into a small and rather tawdry salon, then closed the door and went on down the hall.

Coming to another door, the servant knocked, then entered.

This room was a combination of library and office. A large, flat-topped desk held neat piles of papers and documents, a telephone, a radio receiving set. The room was brilliantly illumined by an electric duster in the ceiling. About the walls stood bookcases, half hidden by large maps outspread and pinned in place. Two chairs stood by the desk.

At the desk sat a man, with Connor's card lying before him. He was of medium height and build and wore loose English tweeds. His hands were large, powerful, with square-ended fingers. His face was delicately outlined and unimpressive, until one observed the heavy brow and piercing eyes; those eyes were cold, unwinking, reptilian, in their deadly regards.

"Well?" he said curtly.

"They have certain mutual business," said the servant, "but each one desires to see you in private, afterward. The son of Han, I do not know. The foreign devil is the same who arrived here last night by air. He carries a portfolio."

"Yes, these men must always carry their papers in something," said Wang Yin, his lip curling in disdain. "Search them. If they carry any weapon, detain them and advise me. If not, admit them at once."

His hand went out to three push-buttons set in a holder on the desk. He touched one and looked up. A picture between two bookcases, on the opposite wall, slid away to reveal the face of a man in the opening.

"Close the opening," said Wang Yin, "unless I signal you. In that case, be ready to shoot if necessary."

The picture slid back into place. A moment later there was a knock at the door, and Connor and Tsing Fan were shown into the room. They had been searched. Wang Yin rose and bowed.

"Come in, gentlemen," he said, and motioned to the two chairs. "I am very glad to see you, Mr. Connor. I have been expecting you ever since your visit with Mr. Sung this morning."

CHAPTER III

CONNOR'S LAST TRUMP

CONNOR GAVE no sign of his startled surprise at these words. He was prepared for Wang Yin's perfect mastery of English, for his shrewdness, for his enmity—but he was not prepared to find his business with Sung known to this man.

He bowed slightly and advanced to the desk, laid down the brief case, and with a smiling word of thanks accepted a cigar from the box Wang Yin extended. Tsing Fan refused, and seated himself.

Wang Yin spun a lighter and Connor accepted it.

"So you keep an eye on Sung, do you?" he asked pleasantly.

Wang Yin nodded, and selected a cigar for himself.

"Naturally," he rejoined. "I am curious to know why you saw him before you saw me, if you come from Mukden. You have references, no doubt."

"Yes." Connor rose and stepped to the desk, and started to unbuckle the brief case. Wang Yin had resumed his chair, almost beside him there. "Certain British officials asked me to see you—but I presume you had best see the letters first."

"By all means," said Wang Yin dryly.

Connor was not anxious for any verbal sparring. He was only too well aware that a word too much, an incautious phrase, would spoil everything; also, there was the subconscious influence, the telepathy, which would certainly give Wang Yin warning within another moment or two.

So, laying down his cigar, he opened the brief case and thrust in his hand as though to bring out his papers. He saw Tsing Fan calmly leave his chair and start toward the wall switch.

Wang Yin caught the movement, and sent a glance at the Chinese.

Connor caught out the slung shot and struck, swift as a flash. Wang Yin's fingers had almost reached the three push-buttons on the desk; they fell limp and then trailed off the polished wood and fell, as Wang's head sagged forward. At the same instant the room was plunged into darkness.

For a moment Connor held his breath, listening, then he relaxed.

"All right; switch 'em on," he said. "He was reaching for those push-buttons. No doubt he meant to signal whomever was watching the room."

"He who treads on the tiger's tail," said Tsing Fan with a chuckle, "does well not to neglect precautions. We took the chance; it is well."

The lights clicked on again.

Connor looked distastefully at the man he had struck down; such a blow smacked of treachery, and revolted him. Yet he knew it had been vitally necessary. In no other manner could he have done his work—and he was striking, not for himself, but to destroy the tentacles that threatened to grip the un-counted thousands of yellow men in a clenching grapple of death and ruin.

"Empty his pockets, take him over into the corner and tie him up," he ordered. "Make some sort of a gag, too, that will keep him from shouting."

"And the knife? Is it not better?" Tsing Fan, holding his wickedly carved blade, made an eager gesture.

Connor frowned. "We are not murderers. Do as I say."

Tsing Fan lifted the senseless Wang Yin from the chair. Connor reached out for the papers piled so neatly on the desk— and at this instant the telephone rang.

THE TWO men exchanged one startled look. Then Connor dropped into the chair and put out his hand to the combined receiver and mouthpiece on its rack. In their brief conversation he had noted the voice of Wang Yin; despite his perfect English, the man spoke with the peculiar singing note of the upper-class Chinese, the soft modulation of voice that denoted one accustomed to speaking pure Mandarin.

"Hello!" he said in English, aping that voice so far as he could.

"This is your servant Lung speaking," came the reply in the same language.

Connor perceived instantly that luck was with him. Evidently Wang Yin used English wherever possible, as in Yunnan City it was seldom spoken.

"The secretary of the governor is here at my house," went on Lung. "He is ready to use the poison to-morrow at noon. I called you to make certain,"

"One moment," said Connor.

In a flash he perceived the chance that was given him, and fought for self-control. So grim old Governor Yuan was to be poisoned—the coup was set for the morrow! Everything else was swept overboard. Connor realized now with full force that he must act in Chinese fashion, with supreme disregard for anything except the winning of the game.

"Lung!" he said, carefully imitating the intonation and the English accent of Wang Yin. "I have just learned that his secretary is playing us false. He has already betrayed us. Have him killed at once, instantly!"

"It will be done, master," came the response.

Connor thrilled exultantly—this man suspected nothing.

"Warn the others that they are to be seized at midnight," went on Connor. Glancing up, he saw the eyes of Tsing Fan fixed upon him, startled, distended. Evidently Tsing Fan understood English. "Troops are being moved out. We are unable to strike now. The traitor has given a list of names, most of us are known. Warn every one to leave the city within half an hour. Go to Wuting-chow, and I will be there to-morrow night."

"As ordered, master," came the emotionless response. Evidently, the men who served Wang Yin were surprised at nothing. "Shall the man be killed slowly?"

"No. Waste no time."

Connor laid the instrument on its rack and drew a deep breath.

"You understood?"

"Yes. I speak English," said Tsing Fan quietly.

"The governor's secretary was to poison Yuan at noon to-morrow."

Comprehension flashed in the dark, oblique eyes.

"And you have ordered him killed!" Tsing Fan broke into a laugh; the laugh of the Chinese, to whom a touch of cruelty appeals strongly. "Excellent! And the others will flee?"

"This man Lung suspected nothing," said Connor. "We have the chance to destroy the whole plot at one blow, from the inside."

Tsing Fan bent over the figure of Wang Yin and completed his task. Rising, he placed on the desk the articles taken from Wang Yin's pockets; money, a few letters, nothing else. Connor placed the letters aside, with the other papers on the desk, which he swiftly gathered together.

The telephone rang again, and he picked up the instrument.

"Hello!"

"Master, this is Yo Chow!" came at thin voice in Chinese. "Lung sent me word—I wish to know whether it is true! If there has been some mistake—"

"The only mistake is your folly in not obeying instantly," said Connor, and gave Tsing Fan a grin.

"Very well. Forgive me, master."

Connor replaced the instrument with a chuckle. He turned his attention to the drawers of the desk, glancing through the papers there, and adding some to the pile set aside.

Tsing Fan, meantime, went to the walls and inspected them narrowly.

"This house," he observed, "belonged to the French collector of customs who killed himself last year. He was a great scoundrel; he took bribes, kept many women, was said to have had secret hiding places in the house."

Connor paid no attention, for he had come upon a number of letters and documents bearing the Soviet symbol, though written in Russian, of which he knew very little. He drew the brief case to him and began to cram these and the other papers into it.

Tsing Fan came to the picture high on the wall between the two bookcases, opposite the desk. It was a small French color-print, set in a frame without glass. Tsing Fan touched it, and found it did not move. He examined it more carefully, and perceived that it was solid in the wall, apparently. He tapped it sharply with his fingers, then again. His knife flashed up and he drove it into the center of the picture with all his force.

Connor looked up, startled; a frightful sound had burst upon the room, like the gasping groan of a dying man. He saw the long knife of Tsing Fan still fixed firmly in the picture, then Tsing pointed to it with an exultant word. Connor saw something dark appear on the surface of the picture, spread upon it, then drip down the wall in a steady red smear.

"He heard me tap, put down his ear to listen—and that was all," said Tsing Fan. "The picture is on a panel of wood."

Reaching up, he made an effort, and the knife came away in his hand with a rush of blood.

"The devil!" exclaimed Connor, starting to his feet. His forgotten cigar was burning the desk-edge, the varnish smelling evilly. "Tsing, we've done the job; now to get out of here. Not a sign of any weapon in the desk, unfortunately. Can we reach Governor Yuan by telephone?"

"No," said Tsing Fan. "He is old style and refuses to have telephones in the palace. We must get out by carving a way with the knife, I think."

Connor nodded. "Looks like it." He buckled shut his bulging brief case and caught up the slung shot. "All right, let's go."

Tsing Fan drew open the door, which opened into the room. The lighted hallway outside was empty, but the two men stared in abrupt dismay and consternation; the doorway opening was completely closed by a steel grille.

CHAPTER IV

THE INQUISITION

CONNOR CLOSED the door swiftly, quietly. "There's been no alarm," he said. "Probably this was some gadget devised by Wang Yin to keep any one from leaving the room except at his signal. Try the windows."

Tsing Fan pulled back one of the heavy draperies cloaking the windows, then let it fall again.

"Barred on the outside," he said briefly.

"Stand by, then. See what happens." Connor went to the desk and pressed the three push-buttons, one after the other.

A click sounded from the wall. The split panel with its picture moved aside, to let a small deluge of blood down the wall; the skull of a Chinese showed in the opening, motionless. Tsing Fan went to the door, opened it slightly.

"The steel is gone!" he exclaimed. "Come quickly!"

One of those three buttons had released the sliding grille outside. Another had slid away the wall panel. But the third—

Connor stepped to the door and switched off the light in the room. With brief case and slung shot, he followed Tsing Fan out into the hall, and closed the door. No one was in sight. For an instant, Connor felt the heart-leap of victory. Already Tsing Fan was at the door opening on the *porte-cochère,* plucking at it—but vainly.

"Locked!" he exclaimed.

And at this instant, the house was plunged into darkness. A thin, shrill cry filled the air; Connor felt the reverberation of naked feet thudding on the hall floor. He threw himself sidewise. Something struck him with fearful force and hurled him headlong, the brief case flying from his grip. It was gone. A figure stumbled over him, a shrill voice cried out. Then Connor was up, on his feet, lashing out blindly with the slung shot. There was a tremendous crash of bursting glass from the door.

The third push-button had brought the avalanche upon them!

A body struck against Connor, gripped him; the slung shot cracked home, there was a scream, he was free again. A terrific uproar was going up all around. Recollecting that there had been side doors from the hall, Connor groped for one, found it, swung it open—and the ray of an electric torch picked him up as he was closing it. There was an instant yell. Bodies came crashing against the door. They were after him, had seen him.

He released the door abruptly. It flew back against him, hurled him against the wall, concealed him perfectly, as men hurtled into the room. Chinese voices filled his ears. The torch ray stabbed about. Then, suddenly as it had gone off, the house light was switched on again. From somewhere lifted a thin, piercing, metallic voice screaming in rage. Connor knew instinctively it was the voice of Wang Yin.

The din quieted. Connor heard the men around him ebb out of the room.

"Both of them gone!" cried a voice that pierced him. "Fools—outside! Comb every inch of the compound and find them! Do not hesitate to shoot."

Wang Yin was in charge, then. Connor gently shoved the door, and discovered that he was in the same salon where they had waited when they had first come in. The room blazed with light. So Tsing had escaped! That was what the bursting glass had meant—he must have gained the gardens outside.

The door closed, Connor snapped off the lights, crossed

hastily to the one window, and drew the curtain aside. An iron grille on the far side of the glass greeted him, and he let the drapery fall again. Even if Tsing Fan had got away, the brief case with its precious freight was gone. Failure weighed heavily upon him. After all, he should have let Tsing put a knife into Wang Yin when they had him. Nothing else would insure the destruction of the man's infernal schemes.

What to do now? Connor thought swiftly, desperately. They were all outside seeking Tsing Fan—ah! Audacity, the one thing they would never expect; and why not? He had bungled things miserably. Why not seize the chance to repair everything? Wang Yin would have found the brief case, would of course take it back into his workroom—

HIS BRAIN thus racing, Connor darted across to the door, opened it, looked out. By the shattered entrance door, now ajar, sprawled the black-clad figure of one of the servants, eloquent testimony that Tsing Fan's knife had found one mark, at least. No one else. The hall was empty. His brief case was gone, of course.

Connor turned toward the room he had so lately left, slung shot in hand. A sudden outburst of voices welled up from outside, instinct with savage ferocity. He came to the office door, and found that the steel grille was not in place.

"We have found him!" came a voice from outside. "We have him, master!"

Another instant and they would be back in the house. Tsing Fan was lost, then. Connor flung open the door before him and darted into Wang Yin's office, slamming the door again.

Wang Yin was not here. Save for the crown of the dead Chinaman in the wall aperture, the room was empty. Nor was there any sign of the brief case.

From the hall sounded the thudding of feet, the shrill sound of excited voices. Battling down his keen dismay, Connor remembered the accident that had saved him, and with two quick strides was behind the door, where it would open against him. A hand rattled the knob, shoved the door partly open.

"He is dead?" asked the voice of Wang Yin. "I see that he is. By the ten hells! This man has no mustache."

"Here is a false one that we found in the hall, master," said another.

The telephone rang stridently, insistently.

"Take his body into another room. Search it and bring me whatever you find," said Wang Yin hastily. He entered the room, slammed the door shut, leaped to the desk and seized the telephone. "Hello!" he said in English.

Tsing Fan dead, then!

Connor took a step forward, then another. Wang Yin leaned over the desk, back to him, and emitted a sudden blasting torrent of oaths. He was just learning about the orders that had been issued in his name, evidently. He had laid an automatic pistol on the desk when he seized the instrument.

"Wait a minute—wait!" he exclaimed. "There is something wrong—"

Connor shoved a thumb into his back.

"Drop it!" he commanded. "Hands up—quick, you devil!"

Wang Yin twisted about, caught a glimpse of Connor's face, and without hesitation dropped the instrument and lifted his arms, his features contorted with fury and dismay.

"Don't try any tricks or you'll stop hot lead," said Connor, and reaching past him, took the automatic from the desk. It was loaded, the safety catch off. He stepped back a pace and grinned cheerfully at the reptilian ferocity of the other man's expression.

"Now put the telephone on the rack—quick, damn you!"

Connor's eyes hardened. Wang Yin reached out and replaced the instrument, staring fixedly at Connor. The latter backed around to the other side of the desk.

"Where's my brief case?" he demanded. The yellow man looked blank.

"Whose game are you playing, Mr. Connor?" he asked slowly. Connor ignored the question and glanced around. No sign of the brief case anywhere. Wang Yin had not brought it back into the room with him—perhaps he did not realize its importance. Across those venomous saffron features flitted a swift glance of understanding.

"Oh!" said Wang Yin. "I see now. It was you who gave those orders they just called me about—I suppose Lung telephoned me and you were clever enough—yes, yes! You're no fool. And the man with you, pretending to be from the Canton government—just who was he, if you please?"

"You might find that out for yourself," said Connor crisply, "since you've killed him."

"As you thought you had killed me, eh?" Wang Yin lifted a hand to his head, his eyes flitting about the room. "Well, you fooled me; I admit it freely. Still I must insist that you assuage my curiosity. Where did you learn so much? Who sent you?"

DESPERATELY, CONNOR cursed the lost brief case. He dared not mention it again lest Wang Yin discover its import; without it, however, now that Tsing Fan was dead, he did not want to leave here. Then Wang Yin started violently, and his eyes widened.

"So—my papers—everything! You foreign devil, who sent you here?"

"China," said Connor calmly. "Your whole scheme is known, Wang. You expected to double-cross the French—"

A spasm of frightful and unutterable rage contorted the yellow features.

"So that's it—I might have known! Those cursed French devils—ah! I was warned not to trust them! I might have known they merely waited a chance of betraying me somehow! Where are my papers gone? Spy! Assassin! Where are they?"

Suddenly Connor sensed something amiss—felt the intangible yet powerful flow of thought from the other man. Wang Yin was sparring for time, was deliberately play-acting a rôle, for some reason. And he remembered the hole in the wall. With a swift feeling almost of panic, he stepped aside, glanced up at the aperture. The head of the dead man was no longer there.

"Hands up, Wang!" he exclaimed, lifting the pistol. "Go to the door—there'll be a pistol in your back now, not my thumb! And if any one shoots me, my finger will contract on the trigger. Step out! You'll take me out of here, anyhow, papers or no papers."

He strode around the desk as he spoke, grim purpose in his eyes, half wishing that Wang Yin would give him an excuse to fire. The other man read his look aright, and without protest turned and raised his hands and went to the door. Connor thrust the pistol-muzzle into the yellow man's back and reached around him, opening the door an inch.

"Pull it open yourself and march to the entrance!"

They stepped out into the hall. No one was in sight except one of the black-clad servants, by the outer door. He straightened up, staring at them.

"Be silent, or your master dies!" Connor spat at him viciously. "If we—"

Connor heard nothing, caught no glimpse of the man who had appeared behind him in the hall, was given no warning whatever; all his attention was fastened upon the servant by the door. A hand reached around from behind him, struck his wrist a smart blow, and at the same instant a crashing impact came against his skull.

The pistol fell from his hand, unfired, as he crumpled up.

WHEN CONNOR regained his senses, his head was aching badly and he had an egg-sized lump over one ear. Also, his wrists were handcuffed together.

He lifted his head and stared around. He was in a corner of Wang Yin's office; Wang sat at the desk, speaking rapidly into the telephone. Two of the black-clad servants stood beside the desk; beside them dangled a half-inch line, depending from a stout hook in the ceiling. Another guard stood over Connor, and seeing the latter move, thrust a rifle-butt into his ribs as a significant hint to be quiet.

"And get here as quickly as you can, Lung!" Wang Yin was saying. "No help for the damage that is already done; we must guard against further harm. It's midnight now, so make haste."

Midnight! Then he must have been unconscious for a considerable time, thought Conner dully. He was aware that Wang Yin had left the telephone and was standing looking down at him, but cared not. The pain in his head was intolerable, and a deeper hurt ached within him. He had failed, miserably and totally. All that he had accomplished was the death of Tsing Fan. If he had given the latter his way, Wang would now be dead and the game won, but his inhibitions had overpowered him.

The two guards leaned over, seized him by the arms, jerked him to his feet. Wang Yin regarded him coldly, calmly.

"I ask you for the last time, my friend: Where are the documents you took?"

Connor was bewildered.

"How do I know?" he rejoined hopelessly. Wang leaned forward, struck him across the face.

"You will soon remember, then! You hid them somewhere. When you have hung for an hour and your body is disjointed, perhaps your memory will waken, eh? String him up."

That blow in the face wakened Con-nor, lashed him to action. His wrists were bound, his arms held—but his foot flashed out in a swift kick that caught Wang Yin under the chin and knocked him sprawling. Instantly Connor was seized and held motionless. With a scream of rage, Wang struggled to his feet, one hand at his throat, then got himself under control and made a gesture.

One of Connor's hands was freed from the handcuffs, he was forced to stand on a chair, and about his free wrist was bound the cord. The chair was withdrawn and he was left hanging by the right arm, his feet well off the floor. One of the servants appeared with an iron weight. This, by means of a cord, was attached to his left ankle, and he spun about slowly in the air, his distended eyes vainly seeking some aid, some release from the weight. Soon, he realized, his arm and leg would be out of the socket, his body disjointed.

"You will remember, yes?" said Wang Yin, regarding him with a thin smile. "After an hour, it will be the other arm and leg, my friend. Oh, yes, I think you will remember."

Taunting, jeering cruelly, he forgot the lesson just given him and came close. Connor spun slowly about—then his left arm whipped out. The handcuffs on his wrist slapped across the face of Wang Yin, and Connor laughed as the infuriated man staggered back.

AT THIS instant came the bursting crack of a pistol shot, outside.

A yell followed, then another—wild, shrill screams instinct with alarm and terror. Wang Yin stood as though paralyzed, in the act of wiping the blood from his cut face; he turned toward the door, listening, thunderstruck. One of the three servants darted out of the room with a cry of inquiry. As he passed through, the door, there came a shot in the hall and the man pitched forward.

Wang Yin leaped into life, uttered a hoarse cry, hurled himself at the desk, trying to reach the spring that would close the sliding door of steel bars.

He was a fraction of an instant too slow.

Connor, literally being torn asunder, racked with spasmodic agony as his muscles slowly gave under the strain, glimpsed a rush of figures in the hall. Three of them came hurtling into the room. Then the steel grille clanged into place, one of the servants slammed the door.

A shot burst out, and another. One of the three uniformed figures was down under the knife of a servant. The other, pistol out, shot the other servant, but pitched forward as the weapon in Wang Yin's hand exploded. The third intruder, who had stumbled and fallen headlong, came to his feet just as Connor, slowly revolving on his cord, turned about and came face to face with him.

This third figure was Tsing Fan.

Connor saw it happen, all in the veriest fraction of a moment, as he slowly spun, helpless. Tsing Fan uprose like a ghost, and the pistol in his hand jerked sharply, twice. To the reports, Wang Yin whirled, flung out his arms, stood there for an instant with the utter ferocity of a wild beast in his face, his eyes blazing hatred and venom. Then, a rush of blood coming from his lips, the life fled out of his eyes and he collapsed.

Tsing Fan leaped to the desk, slashed at the cord with his knife, and Connor, with a sense of blessed relief, felt himself caught and lowered. A moment later, the weight cut from his left leg, he dropped into a chair and stared at the man before him. From the door came a frantic, insistent hammering and pounding. The uniformed Chinese, having finished his opponent, flung open the door, and Tsing Fan put out a hand to the push-buttons and released the steel grille. Figures came bursting into the room.

"You!" Connor gripped the hand of Tsing Fan as the latter came to him again. "Is it real? They said—you were killed in the garden."

"It was one of our men there, spying," said Tsing Fan. "I had posted him there—had not told you. He was the only one I could depend on, and—well, what matter? Your brief case struck me in the darkness. I seized it and got outside. He helped me get away, but they caught him before he could follow over the wall. I went straight to the governor's palace and laid everything before Yuan. He is here, himself."

There was a sudden silence.

Connor looked up, and from the pictures he had seen, recognized the grim old governor who had held Yunnan so firmly in his grip during the years of chaos. Yuan reached out a hand to him and gripped Connor's fingers.

"My friend," said Yuan, "I owe you and others a great deal, but my chief debt is to you. With the documents you obtained, Yunnan is safe from any foreign domination; I have evidence that will hold these vultures back from further attempts."

The impulsive, hearty grip wrenched Connor's arm. A spasm of pain shot through him, and his head fell forward. But, as his eyes closed, there was a smile upon his lips.

The game was won.

VI

THE KING MAKERS

*The last of a long line of emperors stages
a comeback under Yankee auspices.*

CONNOR HAD dressed for dinner, and was rather impatiently awaiting the return of Stanley. It was nearly eight, and time to dine. From his open window he listened to the occasional outburst of rifle or machine-gun fire, coming from the Japanese settlement. Luxurious as it was, the Tientsin Club was beholding parlous times.

Earl Stanley, the booming, raucous-voiced, energetic lawyer from San Francisco, was one of the few men who knew the truth about Connor.

To Tientsin at large, Connor was merely a pleasant young man who had inherited vast financial interests in China, who played polo, raced horses, spent his money languidly, and on the whole was quite an ass. To a very few on the inside, he was known as an energetic young man who mixed largely in political affairs—not for his own interest, but for the good of China.

Tonight he was worried about Stanley, who had no business running around town by himself; while entirely capable, even to speaking Chinese, Stanley was a stranger in Tientsin and had only recently come on a visit from San Francisco. For Japan had occupied Mukden, was seizing all Manchuria in her grasp, and China was in the throes of wild and ineffectual protest. From the native city, bandits and alleged patriots had flooded into the Japanese quarter of Tientsin to kill and rob. Native mobs were being shot down, and all Tientsin was in alarm and uproar.

The telephone jangled sharply. Connor picked up the instrument, and heard the voice of the missing.

"Connor? Stanley speaking. Say, I'm over in the French settlement, in Rue Favier—a small restaurant called the Rendezvous des Tirailleurs, close to Rue Gros. You can't miss it. Get here quick as a taxi can roll you. Fetch along my traveling cap and a pair of pants."

"Excellent!" Connor chuckled. "Why not a pair of slippers?"

"Hey, this is no joke!" came the response, sharply urgent. "Police been after me yet?"

"No."

"This is something big. Get here on the jump, will you?"

"Sure thing."

"And, say! Bring along some Chinese chap you can trust, will you?"

"Right."

CONNOR GOT the club desk on the wire and found that his car and chauffeur were on hand. Catching up Stanley's cap and an odd pair of trousers, he rolled them up hastily, left his room, and two minutes later was stepping into his car beside the driver, a rotund little Szechuan man named Wang, who was absolutely devoted to him.

He was soon rolling down Victoria Road toward the French settlement. A far, thin sound of rifle-fire came from the Japanese quarter ahead, then was hushed. Connor knew that Stanley must be in some sort of a mess, which was nothing new. Since his arrival in China, Earl Stanley had been thrusting his eager head into all kinds of trouble, from which he seemed to emerge by a miracle without great damage.

The police, Connor noted, were out full force, and files of troops were marching through the streets. There was no danger outside of the Japanese quarter, however. The car swung down Hsinyuen Road and angled off through the French settlement to its destination, which was a small, very ordinary, none too

high grade restaurant. Telling Wang to park the car and follow him, Connor strode in.

A few people were in evidence. There was no sign of Stanley in sight. The proprietor came up, rubbing his hands, and Connor asked a question. The Frenchman opened his eyes wide.

"Ah! It is M'sieu Connor! Come with me, m'sieu. In the private room off the balcony. Your friend is discussing business. There is some excellent Vouvray, m'sieu, actually of the '21 vintage! And dinner has been awaiting your arrival."

"Serve it, then," said Connor curtly. Wang followed him, and the French, who never ask questions and are surprised at nothing, paid no heed.

From a small balcony at the rear, opened a private room of some size. The proprietor knocked and flung open the door with a flourish. Connor stepped in. Wang followed him and closed the door. Then, after one slack-jawed stare of utter astonishment the chubby Wang slipped down on his knees, put his palms on the floor, and bowed his head between them.

Connor saw the action, but failed to comprehend it for a moment. He looked at Stanley, brawny, breezy, in great good humor, who was talking with a native; a young Chinese who wore black-rimmed spectacles, his features rather weak. He was oddly attired in a heavy sweater pulled over a native robe. Something vaguely familiar about his face struck Connor, but he could not place the man.

"Hello! Attaboy! Good work!" Stanley leaped to his feet with a sudden laugh. "So you don't recognize my pal, eh? He understands English but prefers Mandarin. Don't know him?"

The native met Connor's frowning gaze, and smiled.

"When we last met," he said in purest Mandarin, "I was not wearing these clothes."

"Good lord!" exclaimed Connor in amazement. Then he bowed. "A surprise indeed, your—"

"Shut up! Sit down!" barked Stanley. "Wang, you fool, get up! Connor, we're all in one hell of a fix. So is Henry, here. Call him Henry, for the love of mike! Here's the waiter."

Not one waiter, but two, who brought an excellent meal and with it a couple of bottles of Vouvray. Connor lit a cigarette and appeared at his ease. Wang stood stiffly in one corner, a trace of fear in his eyes. Stanley spoke in rapid English, using as much slang as possible; he knew that Frenchmen never speak English but always understand it.

"You're wise now, are you? All right. I met up with this bird a few blocks away, at the edge of the Jap quarter. Hell of a fuss going on over there, a lot of shooting. This gazebo was looking pretty dazed. No one about, luckily. Come to find out, he'd had a row with the little brown brothers. Don't know why as yet. Some sons of T'ang had shown up with bombs, too. He's got a bullet-hole in his coat and was scared stiff. I bet the Japs are moving heaven and earth right now to find him, too. His establishment was in their settlement, you know."

Connor nodded. "Why did you speak of the police?"

"Well, a Jap officer came along. This guy started to run and the Jap got nasty, so I pasted him good and hard. They'll get me by the description, sooner or later. I shoved this bird along and landed him here. Safe enough. Didn't dare go anywhere else."

CONNOR'S KEEN, tensed features were immobile, but he said nothing until the waiters had departed.

He needed those few moment to recover from the abrupt shock. He was inwardly stunned, incredulous, doubting his own senses. This young native in the sweater and spectacles was Henry Chang-yin. He was the last of the line of the great Nurhachu, founder of the Manchu empire, and the throne of the Yellow Dragon was his by rights.

Exiled like the other Manchu princes, Hsuan, as he was usually termed, had lived in retirement in the Japanese settlement, supported by the Japanese. He was a quiet sort, without great force, educated by English tutors. The sons of T'ang, the republican Chinese of the north, hated and feared him as being the rightful emperor, a pawn waiting in the hand of Japan.

All this leaped across Connor's mind in a flash, all this and more. With an effort, however, he kept himself under control. Like a man who has found some great pearl in the gutter, he feared for an instant lest destiny were mocking him. Then, like a flash of fire speeding through his veins, he accepted the sudden swift gamble. He saw a dozen things he could do, great things, daring things. Here in his hand, for his own use—if he could hold it—was the pawn whose move could shake the entire Oriental world.

The door closed, the waiters ware gone. Connor drew a deep breath and gave Stanley a look.

"I understand about the coat and pants now. Well, who's running the show?"

"What d'you mean?" demanded Stanley, his wide, forceful features wrinkled up in a frown. "What show?"

"This," said Connor. "All of it. You and I can't both run it. We have different notions."

Before the lawyer could reply, Hsuan leaned forward, gravely.

"My friends, I am hungry. Abandon formality and let us eat," he said. "From this moment I become Henry, nothing else. Who is this son of Han? Let him sit with us."

This was shrewd enough, as Connor realized. Wang was indeed a son of Han, a Chinese of the south. This Henry was no fool, then!

The alert and hungry emperor who had no throne, insisted that they pitch into the meal, and himself set the example. Connor soon understood that he was suspicious of everything around him, and quite timid. Between bites, he spoke freely, and in naive fashion laid before them a singular and alarming situation. Connor, whose brain was already driving far out and around, probing a dozen possibilities, began to feel his head very loose on his shoulders. Stanley had picked up a whole package of dynamite, which might send them all up together at any moment.

"My friends," said the spectacled native, "the Japanese are determined to take me to Manchuria. They want to make me emperor in Mukden, to rule for them. I do not wish it. I am comfortable, happy, peaceful. They threatened, bribed, tempted me to go. When the chance came tonight, I ran away.

"But now, what? I have nowhere to go. I can trust nobody at all. Can I trust you? I do not know. Everybody I trusted has betrayed me. Tonight the Chinese came to kill me. I have no money. I have nothing. I am not safe anywhere. The only man I could trust absolutely is old Jung Tien, the former mandarin, who keeps a shop in the native city. He has a few former red bannermen of his own clan, who would serve me faithfully. But how can I reach them? I do not know my way. I am helpless."

Indeed, the man was pitifully helpless. He was caught in the net of destiny. This last of a great and able line was terrified by the very thought of becoming a puppet emperor in the city that had produced his ancestors.

THE MANCHURIAN bannermen throughout China, exclusively warriors in the days of the empire, had been dispersed or slaughtered when the empire was overthrown. He had no party, no backing. He had behind him only the loyalty of a few scattered men. He could trust no one, and he had no future.

Having said all he had to say, having spoken out his feeble soul, he ate and drank avidly. Stanley leaned forward and put his hand on Connor's arm, his brown, vigorous features all alight, his voice lowered.

"Connor, I see what you mean about running the show. Well, you are! It's your party. You do whatever seems best to you, and count on me to stand by."

For an instant Connor's quick, warm smile flashed out, then was gone again. Excitement was rising high within him. Here was indeed something to fire his imagination! And, his hunger somewhat appeased, he began to speak.

He had not touched the wine, yet he was stirred out of himself, lifted to far heights. The greenish-gold wine was, however, quite extraordinary. As Stanley observed, only vintners could tell why the best Vouvray is frequently found in the worst restaurants. Henry partook of it freely, and his dull eyes brightened, and animation crept into his cheeks.

"Let's look at the situation sensibly," said Connor, with easy familiarity. "You say you've no money, Henry? I thought the Chinese government had been paying you half a million dollars a year?"

"That was the agreement, but they paid nothing," said Henry. "The Japanese have paid for everything."

"Oh!" said Stanley. "Then, in that case, I should think—"

Connor kicked him under the table, and he subsided.

"Don't think, Stanley. Now, what's the situation in the north? Japan wants Manchuria and practically has it. The League of Nations will flutter like a lot of old women. Japan will nominally back down, but will leave Manchuria in the hands of her own puppets. That is, unless actual war ensues. Anything's possible. Japan will set up a new government in Manchuria. The Chinese won't dare fight, for their whole government has gone smash. So Japan wins—except for the three of us sitting here!

She ought to win, too. The Chinese cannot govern themselves. Now, listen to me, Henry! If you say the word, we'll go!"

The keen eyes of Connor were narrowed, alight, dancing eagerly. Stanley watched them with delight, perhaps guessing what thoughts were racing through the agile brain.

"Where will we go?" asked Henry, blinking.

"To glory or the devil!" and Connor laughed. "What do you care? You're the last of the Tsing dynasty, who came out of Mukden and carved themselves an empire. Half of China is republican and hates you, the other half wants a man, a leader, a name, and will erupt like a volcano if he appears. You are the volcano, Henry!

"Appear suddenly in Manchuria, alone, with no Jap backing. Proclaim yourself, and what happens? Thousands of men will join you overnight. There'll be a storm of men in the north, such as hasn't been seen since Nurhachu threw his horde over the Great Wall! You've nothing to lose, everything to win. We'll get you into Manchuria—"

"How?" asked Henry. A touch of color had risen in his face. He reached for the Vouvray and refilled his glass. "Not by train. That's impossible. And—"

"By ship, of course. Leave that to me." Connor brushed aside the query. "General Ma and whatever is left of the army up there, will gather behind you like a shot. The Japs have broken him now; he'll do anything to save face!"

"But we happen to be in Tientsin," put in Stanley. "And no use blinking it—the Jap secret service is a wow! They won't lose any time picking up Henry's trail. That's why I told you to bring a native with you. You take Henry off, leave your friend Wang— he'll pose as the native who came here with me. Get the idea?"

Connor nodded. "Right. Henry, get into those pants. Give Wang your spectacles."

"I can't see without them!" exclaimed the Manchu plaintively.

"You don't need to see. You'll come with me. Stanley, if the

Japs do run you down, face it out. Wang is a splendid liar. He's the chap you met, and so forth. Cover up. Get me?"

"Right." Stanley nodded coolly. "And where'll you be?"

"Getting backing. Money, men, supplies." Connor swung about to the Manchu, who was climbing into the trousers. He abandoned his jocular manner and swung into grave, sonorous Mandarin. "Your Majesty! Great Maternal Ancestor! Do you agree! If you say the word, we'll carry you to a throne in Manchuria, the throne of your ancestors—and you'll stand for yourself!"

"What will you get out of it?" asked Henry, reaching for his wine-glass. Connor laughed.

"Nothing. A timber concession, perhaps, if you must give me something."

"Agreed!" Henry straightened up before them. Sudden enthusiasm shook the slight, irresolute figure. The loose mouth tightened, a flash leaped in the dark eyes. "Agreed! Not a puppet, but a real ruler? Agreed! Yes! The lowered flag will go up again. The Manchus will have an emperor. It is agreed! I have heard of you. They say you are honest. I will do what you say!"

Connor lifted his untouched glass.

"Agreed, then. To Hsuan, emperor of Manchuria, ruler of the Manchus!" His voice chimed on the room like a bronze bell. There was a click of clinking glasses, then Connor flung his own against the wall and came to his feet with the crash.

"Ready? Henry, come along with me. Back at the Tientsin Club in an hour, Stanley."

"Maybe." Stanley burst into his booming laugh. "So long! See you in jail!"

CHAPTER II

THE CHINESE city was seething. Students were parading, anti-Japanese mobs were in full swing, orators spouted on every street-corner. Massacre and death were in the air, and all ears listened for further grim drumming of machine-guns from the Japanese settlement.

No one heeded Henry, in slouchy European garb like thousands of others, a cap pulled over his eyes. Connor had left his car, and now piloted the confused Manchu on foot, into the great thoroughfare called Pei-ma-lu. In this street was the shop of Jung Tien, who sold brocades, silks and other materials for ladies' shoes. Henry, who had seldom left his own residential grounds, knew only vaguely where the shop might be.

Fortunately, Connor was quite at home in the bewildering array of medieval signs hanging out before the shops. Presently he saw the oblong vermilion cloth hanging from a yellow bar, that betokened Jung Tien's trade, and on nearing the shop in question, found that eminently Manchu name inscribed beside the door. Like most of those in the street, the shop was open for tourist business, and Connor walked in with his companion.

"I seek the honorable Jung Tien," he said to the shopman who approached. "Henry, remain here and look at materials."

Five minutes later, Connor stood in the rear room. With him was a vigorous, hearty man of seventy years, who had taken one peep out into the shop and then gone ashen gray.

"No time to explain," said Connor. "Can he remain with you for a day, undetected by those who seek him?"

"Yes, of course," stammered old Jung. "The son of heaven—"

"His name is Henry, and he is a student. Tomorrow night we depart for Manchuria. There the emperor Hsuan proclaims himself—if he's not found first. Half a dozen Manchu bannermen to accompany him. Can do?"

The old eyes flashed. "Yes! My grandson Jung Toy will lead them."

"Once there, can men and money be expected?"

"Men? Of course. Money? Yes." Jung eyed him keenly. "I have heard of you. Men say you are a superior man. Hm! Five million China dollars when you reach Manchuria; they are ready now for delivery. Another ten million, as soon as it can be rushed from various cities. Say, ten days."

"Enough," said Connor, with a nod of satisfaction. "The dynasty of Tsing still has faithful supporters, I see! I will send you word where to bring him tomorrow evening."

"How shall I know if the word comes from you?"

Connor laughed. "The messenger will bear Henry's spectacles as a token."

HE LEFT the shop, giving Henry a clap on the shoulder in passing, and so passed out into the street again. His whirlwind visit must have left old Jung Tien in a morass of incredulity; but the old ex-mandarin had spoken up like a man. No doubt some Manchu organization existed, some means of raising men and money quickly if there was any chance of another Tsing reaching a throne.

And meantime, Henry was safely bestowed, with the most faithful of men around him.

Connor caught a tram and headed back for Victoria Road. His first exultation, his wild and fanciful concept, had taken solid form. Now he had realities to face. He saw that getting Henry out of Tientsin by rail was an impossibility, for the Japanese controlled the railroads. The roads at this season were impassable for cars. There remained only the sea route, safest and quickest—even air was out of the question.

"And everything going down the Peiho River will be watched alow and aloft!" thought Connor. "Most of the Manchurian trade is controlled by the Japanese. Hm!"

The more he fronted it, the more acute grew the problem. Getting away by rail or air could be managed, but reaching the other end was the ticklish part. Remained the sea, involving a trip down-river to the Taku anchorage, with Japanese warships, troop ships and spies on every hand. Spies formed the chief obstacle, for they were legion. Not Japanese alone, but Chinese, Koreans, Russians and others. Connor's problem was not in getting away, which might be managed, but in getting away to a particular destination. The obstacles were insuperable. The more he thought about it, the more he realized this.

He walked into the club, found no trace of Stanley, and went on up to his room.

Lighting a cigarette, he smoked it out in vain thought. There were many things he might attempt; the devil of it was, he could not afford to fail! There would be no second chance. He had to win through or go under.

Connor came suddenly to his feet. At this moment the door was flung open to admit Stanley, with Wang at his heels.

"I've got it!" exclaimed Connor excitedly. Stanley slammed the door.

"You have, by gad! They're on to us. You weren't gone five minutes before they showed up. Chap named Honzai, colonel on the general staff. He made me sweat, let me tell you! Connor, how far can these fellows go, anyhow? It's got me worried!"

Connor chuckled. "No doubt. And you're right. What happened?"

"Oh, I bluffed. They're on, but they can't prove anything. They'll be here any minute. I imagine they're getting British law behind 'em."

"Good!" exclaimed Connor. "Wang, clear out, quick! Now, Stanley, when Honzai gets here, let me do the talking. You'll back me up in anything?"

"You bet!" boomed Stanley. "With me at your back, shoot the works!"

So it was agreed.

BEING IN a club, and also in the British settlement, ev-

erything was managed very deftly and without commotion. It
might have been a party of old friends to whom Connor opened
his door. Colonel Honzai was a lean, trim, efficient man of
indeterminate age, whose eyes were very alert behind his spectacles. Whatever were his intentions in bringing two aides and
a pair of English inspectors, he stifled them on being warmly
welcomed by Connor. He promptly agreed to a private confer-
ence, and his party passed into the adjoining room, occupied
by Stanley, The latter closed the door and rejoined Connor and
the Japanese colonel.

"I know why you're here, of course," said Connor cheerfully.
"You're after Henry, eh?"

Colonel Honzai blinked. "You do not evade, sir?"

"Of course not!" exclaimed Connor. "My friend Stanley, here,
is quite out of it. You want Henry, and I've got him. And I'm
the only one who knows just where Henry is."

"This," said the colonel stiffly, "is not the way to speak of
imperial majesty. Respect—"

"Respect be hanged! He's a weak-kneed young man, and
between you and me, he's scared stiff," said Connor, with an air
of confidential frankness. "I promised to help him get away
from Tientsin, and I shall keep my promise."

"Yes?" said Honzai quietly. "I have heard of you, Mr. Connor.
I have even suspected that you might not be exactly what you
appear on the surface—"

"Correct! None of us is," cut in Connor amiably. "Well, I'm
going to help Henry get away, so that's settled. He's not paying
me for it, either. If you interfere, you'd not find him at all. That
would be rather silly, wouldn't it? It would be much better
policy," he added thoughtfully, "if you were to help me get him
away."

Colonel Honzai regarded him steadily for a moment.

"Oh! And where does he desire to go?"

"Anywhere, no matter," said Connor carelessly. "Now, if we

were to take him aboard a ship and put out to sea, the outcome would be simple. That is, if it were worth our while."

COLONEL HONZAI suddenly brightened. "Ah! You would discuss finances?"

"Exactly."

For a moment Colonel Honzai remained silent, but the light in his eyes betrayed inward excitement. Abruptly, he came to his feet.

"You will excuse me for one half-hour? I am a very humble cog in the machine. I shall return, with your permission, and continue the discussion."

"By all means," said Connor cordially. "But, my dear sir, bear just one thing in mind! It is not every day that one catches an emperor. You comprehend?"

White teeth flashed beneath the stubby mustache, and the officer bowed.

"Nippon is not stingy, gentlemen. Good-by for the present."

He gathered up his entire escort and departed. When the door closed behind them, Stanley held a match to his pipe. Over the flame, his eyes drove out at Connor.

"You seem amused."

"I am!" and Connor laughed exultantly, his eyes very eager. "That chap is quivering all over this minute! I fitted things right into his plans! They could ask nothing better than to get Henry away from here quietly, without a fuss, in secret. The news will go out later that he's at sea, bound across the gulf for Dairen and the Manchurian throne! Beautiful! Too late for objections, too late for anything!"

"Hm!" said Stanley drily. "Well, I said it was your show, and I'll back it, sweet or bitter. Everybody else has been selling out that poor devil, so we might as well get our share."

An expression of the utmost amazement leaped into Connor's face. He saw that Stanley was entirely serious.

"Indeed?" he said. "You've no compunction about it, I hope?"

"I'm not letting you down," said Stanley. "I don't like it a damned bit, but I'll not go back on my word. It's the only thing to do, I suppose."

"Absolutely. They'll supply us with some sort of craft. We put to sea with him. A destroyer overhauls us and takes him off—giving us gold in exchange. It's simple."

"Very," said Stanley, with a grimace. "I knew you'd do the one thing that nobody else would dream of doing! Well, I'm going downstairs and write a letter or two."

"Do. Come back when Honzai shows up."

STANLEY DEPARTED. Connor broke into swift laughter, settled down in a chair, and got out his pipe. Wang sidled into the room and departed again at a gesture. Connor was puffing away complacently at his pipe when Stanley returned, bringing Colonel Honzai with him. The latter bowed and accepted the chair Connor offered.

"I can make an offer," he said abruptly, bluntly. "Ten thousand."

"Agreed!" exclaimed Connor warmly. "Ten thousand English pounds—"

"No, no! Wait!" broke in the other with marked agitation. "You mistake! Ten thousand China dollars, is the very top sum I can—"

"Then go back and talk again." Connor leaned back in his chair. "I meant to ask fifty thousand gold dollars, American dollars! The price is now sixty thousand. Within five minutes it becomes seventy-five thousand." He smiled at the staring officer, quite calmly. "There will be no argument, no bartering. You may accept my terms, or adopt your own course. Henry is in Chinese hands, well beyond your reach, and unless I get him away he will probably be killed. I can save him. You cannot. Perhaps you prefer to have him dead?"

Colonel Honzai was more than perturbed. He was stirred to the very bottom of his emperor-adoring soul. Puppet or not, Hsuan was a potential emperor, and he said as much. It was obvious that he did not want the Manchu dead. The pawn on the board was of supreme importance.

"Yet you cannot be in earnest!" he went on, blinking rapidly. "Such a sum—"

"Manchuria is worth it. You want to put him on the throne, don't you?"

"We did yes. What is now planned, I do not know. You will be arrested, you will be—"

"Which won't help you one bit," said Connor. "Sixty thousand. Half in advance. The remainder on delivery. In three minutes the price goes up. Yes or no?"

"Yes. Yes!" The other gulped hard. "You have a plan?"

"Of course. So have you. Thirty thousand tomorrow morning, delivered here. Agreed?"

Colonel Honzai accepted a cigarette.

"Agreed. Then what is your plan?"

"That you provide a small craft with a Chinese crew you can trust. At the Taku anchorage, any time after dark tomorrow evening," said Connor coolly. "We'll come aboard in the course of the evening and sail about midnight. By morning, we'll be at sea, bound south. Your captain may decide upon a course with you. One of your destroyers or other craft can meet us in the morning, and we shall be helpless to resist."

Colonel Honzai relaxed in his chair, and positively beamed on Connor and Stanley.

"Much as I had planned it myself!" he approved. "We must not arouse his suspicions, of course. English officers—hm! Yes, I can arrange that. There is a steam-yacht now available to us at Taku, the *Hokko Naiban.* How will you get down to her?"

"Railroad down to Tangku," said Connor promptly, "then take a launch out to the anchorage off Taku. What assurance have I that we'll not be molested on the way?"

"You may feel safe," was the reply. "We desire no excitement, no commotion. You, sir, are a very astute gentleman. You will understand."

Connor smiled. "It is a pleasure to do business with you, colonel."

The other rose and bowed. "Tomorrow morning you will receive the stipulated sum, also exact information as to reaching the *Hokko Naiban*. That is all? Good night."

Colonel Honzai took his departure, trim and efficient. When he was gone, Connor swung around to Stanley, his eyes blazing with exultation.

"Done!" he exclaimed vibrantly. "Thirty thousand in gold! Can you beat it?"

"Yes, blast you!" said the lawyer bluntly. "With thirty pieces of silver!"

Connor burst into a laugh and caught Stanley in his arms, shaking him.

"Stanley, old chap—and you'd still stick by me! Bully for you! And there's thirty thousand for the emperor's war-fund, a fast boat to get away on, the little brown brothers working hard for us—and won't they be hopping mad when they wake up, eh? Get the point now, do you?"

CHAPTER III

CONNOR HAD few preparations to make, and no one he dared trust.

A messenger arrived at the club next morning with a large packet of bank-notes and word that the launch of the *Hokko Naiban* would be waiting at the Tangku railroad station wharf from eight o'clock until twelve that night, with Captain Farson in command.

Wang, bearing the emperor's spectacles, was sent to the shop of Jung Tien, carrying most of the bank-notes as a contribution to the Manchu's war-chest, and very explicit instructions for Jung Toy—the Talented Jung. Stanley, who was new to China but who had all sorts of legal and illegal friends in shipping circles, was sent after certain essential information. Connor, aware that he was undoubtedly being shadowed, left the club with an air of hurried importance and went to the park, where he sat on a bench for an hour or more, reading the papers.

He returned to his room at the club to find Wang just back. All was well, and the orders would be followed to the letter. Ten minutes later, Earl Stanley showed up, vigorous and breezy and self-confident as ever, thoroughly enjoying his risky intrigue.

"This Farson is a fairly bad egg," he reported. "He was let out by the Burns Philp people a couple of years back. Has been running a China coaster ever since, and last year shifted to a Jap line. An Englishman doesn't go to work for Orientals unless he's pretty far down, as a rule. This yacht in question is a good craft. Belonged to some wealthy Jap who died here two or three months ago, but she's old and out of date. Has been for sale cheap. Suit you?"

"Fine," said Connor. "You're a good investigator. The club is getting us a compartment and four tickets to Tangku this evening. We get there at eight-thirty. If Jung Toy does his part, everything's jake."

"Suppose we get double-crossed?"

"How?"

"I dunno, feller." Stanley grinned. "If this was San Francisco, I could tell you. They might figure we'd double-cross them, and beat us to it."

"Possibly. God gave us brains to meet emergencies, but not enough to foretell the future."

SHORTLY AFTER dark that evening the three of them piled out of a taxicab at the East Station and drew a little apart from the milling throng. They were presently joined by a tall, lean Manchu of forty years, and his servant. Jung Toy exchanged a few words with Connor, then turned away and departed. The servant remained and accompanied them to their compartment, where, with a sign of relief, he donned his black-rimmed spectacles and peered around.

"Are we safe?" he asked. Stanley clapped him on the back.

"As safe as we are, or safer, so cheer up! With us behind you, my boy, your future is assured. Connor is a quiet chap and doesn't expand in true American fashion, but yours truly has no false modesty. We're off on the big play, and we'll push you over or go bust!"

Henry had no more to say during the twenty-seven miles to Tangku Station.

While Connor might have avoided the various changes by having the yacht come upriver to the French settlement wharf, his general scheme would thereby have incurred distinct peril. Until they reached the Taku anchorage off the river mouth. Captain Farson would undoubtedly remain in touch with Honzai's agents.

Both Connor and Stanley were well aware that, even if their entire program succeeded, the future was uncertain. Proclamation of Emperor Hsuan was one thing, establishing him in power would be something else again. To this, Stanley was supremely indifferent, being all set for a splendid and glorious adventure, bubbling over with enthusiasm. Connor's thought was all for the ulterior consequences. He had private information that the entire Chinese government meant to resign. China was in the most complete chaos, and if Manchuria suddenly proclaimed an emperor, the last of the Tsing dynasty, anything would be possible.

"Can't say I think much of our emperor," observed Stanley, as he and Connor went into the passage for a smoke and a breath of air. "You confounded Irish have always picked magnificent morons to follow, from the Stuarts on down the line. However, I suppose it doesn't matter."

"This chap may show up better," said Connor thoughtfully. "Blood will tell, you know. Give this poor devil a chance, and I believe he'll surprise us all."

He was to remember these words later, in a bitter moment.

AT TANGKU Station, they found Captain Farson—a saturnine gentleman with a heavy jaw, who introduced himself, shook hands, and brought up porters. Henry was entirely ignored. At the wharf was a large river-launch hired for the occasion, as Farson explained, and with no delay they were off and chugging down toward Taku and the marshlands. Connor remained on deck with Farson, the others going into the cabin.

"You're fully acquainted with this business, Cap'n?" asked Connor.

"Aye." Farson chuckled. "Rather neat, I call it."

"So I think. You'll sail as soon as we're aboard?"

"Aye. It'll take us two hours to reach the yacht."

"Then I'll get a bit of sleep."

The time dragged. It was close to eleven when the lights of Taku appeared, and a bitter cold night it was; in another three weeks the river would be frozen over for the winter. The lights of several steamers showed across the bar. The launch headed straight for the outermost light, and upon drawing near, Connor perceived that the yacht was no large one. The gangway was out, lights showed.

Chinese seamen and two other white officers waited at the head of the ladder. Galloway, the chief engineer, was a burly man with a black eye and cut-up face, smelling far and wide of rum. Hawkins, first officer, a small man, was mild of feature, apologetic of manner.

"We'll get under way at once," said Farson, after performing the introductions. "Mr. Hawkins, be good enough to show our friends to their cabins."

He started for the ladder. Connor followed him.

"I'll just come along, Cap'n. Want a word with you, if you don't mind."

Farson waited on the bridge, obviously none too well pleased.

"Something I forgot to tell you," said Connor cheerfully. "This chap we're taking off sent a couple of his wives and their servants by launch, down-river from the city. They'll be along at any moment, so we'd better wait."

"Wives!" and Farson snorted. "Man, we want no yellow women aboard!"

"You can't help it," said Connor. "He said they'd be dressed as men, anyhow. It won't hurt to humor him a bit."

Farson gave grudging assent, and called down to leave the gangway as it was.

"Sailing on short notice," he said, "and haven't got the craft shipshape, but the cabins are in fair condition."

"You're cleared for Shanghai?"

Farson hesitated. "No, for Dairen."

Connor shrugged and made no comment. The figure of Stanley appeared on the ladder. Connor, under the overhead light, beckoned him.

"We're double-crossed," he said softly. "As soon as they're aboard and we get under way, cut loose! They'll probably be good and seasick after an hour of this swell—we'll have to act at once. I'll handle the bridge, here. You attend to Hawkins, then take over the engine-room. Tell Wang to sweep the decks with the Manchus, clap every man into the forecastle. Get me?"

"You bet," assented Stanley. "What's up?"

"Don't know yet. Here he comes. Well, how's our friend below?"

"Groaning already," and Stanley chuckled as the captain joined them. "The river-swell finished him. He's turned in, and he'll stay put. Steam up, Cap'n?"

"Aye. Damn the delay! Steward's fetching us up some hot coffee, gentlemen. Better step inside and be comfortable."

They followed him into the pilot-house, where a small table was spread. After a moment Hawkins appeared, was told of the delay, and offered no comment. The yellow steward came with a tray and set out sandwiches and coffee.

Connor knew that if the river-trip had made Jung Toy and his men seasick, as was not unlikely, the game was lost.

THE WAITING was interminable. Farson's dark eyes

studied his two passengers alertly, as though he were sizing them up, preparing for something he knew was coming. Connor understood those glances perfectly, and deliberately put on his gayest and most reckless air.

At length a hail came from the lookout forward. At the bridge rail, Connor looked down as the shape of a launch swept in under the ladder. His voice bit out, and that of Jung Toy made brief answer. He turned to Farson, as Stanley went on down the ladder to meet the arrivals.

"It's our crowd. You're all clear now."

"And high time," said the skipper. "Mr. Hawkins! Take that crowd down and let 'em bunk with their boss or where they like. Then get our hook up and we'll go."

Shrill Chinese voices sounded, a whistle shrilled, the rattle and bang of steam winches echoed across the rolling waters.

Ten minutes later, Connor sat in the bridge house. Farson stood watching the hooded binnacle as the engines sent the *Hokko Naiban* swirling out to sea and the lights behind dropped into the distance. At the steam steering gear stood a Chinese seaman.

"Steady as she goes," ordered Farson, and turned with a sigh of relief. "Well, we're off! You'll not mind a trip to Dairen and back, Mr. Connor?"

"Not in the least," said the latter carelessly. "You don't mean that we're going there?"

"Aye. The plans were changed. Instead of a ship meeting us—what's that?"

From somewhere forward a shrill, high voice shrieked in the night. Connor's hand slipped out his pistol.

"Turn your back," crackled his voice. "Put 'em up—stand quiet!"

CHAPTER IV

THE SHIP was taken. The capture was rapid, if not painless. Galloway looked into Stanley's pistol and submitted like a lamb. Surprisingly enough, the only officer to show fight was little Hawkins, who knocked up Stanley's weapon and drove in like a game-cock. Stanley laughed, knocked him sprawling, and locked him into his own cabin. The steward also put up a battle, firing a fruitless shot at Wang, who promptly knifed him. That was the only shot fired. The eight men in the crew, caught completely by surprise, were rounded up forward and the hood of the forecastle was locked upon them, together with the off watch of the black gang.

Captain Farson remained on the bridge. Jung Toy took up his post in the engine-room, while Stanley mounted to the bridge to report, with Wang trailing him.

"Officers all had gats," said Stanley, "Extra guns in their cabins, too. Our crowd is well armed now."

"Japanese pistols, eh?" said Connor, examining one of the weapons. Captain Farson glowered at them, a flame in his black eyes, danger in his dark features.

"You'll all sweat for this! It's piracy, that's what!"

"True," said Connor. "You're excused, Skipper. Wang, take him below and lock him in his cabin. Watch your step, Farson, for Wang is rather expert with a knife. So long."

They departed. Secure in the knowledge that everyone aboard, except the men feeding the fires, was safely locked up, Connor took up the chart which the skipper had been using, and Stanley peered over his shoulder.

"About a day's run across to Dairen, eh?" said Connor. "They figured it was no use having another craft meet us; that Farson could run over there and land our Manchu friend. Instead, we'll run up north to the head of the gulf, and land there at any fishing village. Then straight over the hills, across the railroad, and the job's done."

"You're far from Mukden, aren't you?" asked Stanley.

"Sure. We need to be, for the Japs are there. Once in the hills, we'll proclaim him and the rest will be like a rolling snowball. Stanley, we've done it! We're headed north now, and this time tomorrow night we'll be somewhere in Manchuria. Congratulations all round!"

"Huh! You've handled it well," and Stanley chuckled. "We ought to haul Henry out and have a celebration, but he's sick. Since the course changed, she's quit rolling. He'll probably be up and around by morning. What's the program? Details, I mean."

"Hm! It's midnight now," said Connor. "We have only to keep heading north; nothing in the way. I'll put Wang at the helm, and the Manchus on guard. You and I grab off some sleep, for we'll be needing it by tomorrow night, when the real work begins."

CONNOR WAS emphatically no seaman, and neither was Stanley. To both of them it appeared that a fairly sensible chap like Wang could keep the yacht headed into the north, especially as he had only to set the steam steering gear and leave it alone. It never occurred to either of them that such things as currents, leeway, and the curiosity of a Chinaman to see how mechanical contraptions worked, might affect their plans.

Thus it happened that the *Hokko Naiban* went tearing full speed ahead under the cold stars, straight up the gulf of Liaotung, hour after hour. Half a dozen Manchus prowled about her decks or hung over her rail, unhappy men. Her officers were locked up. Little Wang had his sweet will with the steam steering gear. Down below, Jung Toy grimly held the luckless stokers at work, poised on the gratings above them like a lean dark fiend in hell.

By grace of the Manchu gods, no lumbering junk was encountered that night. But when Wang sent a hurried summons for Connor at sunrise, imminent disaster threatened. The yacht was a scant two miles off shore, the mountains piling up to port in the sunrise glory, and she was yawing back and forth as Wang tried the lever at different points on the slide. To the northeast was a trail of black smoke lifting against the sunrise sky.

Connor dashed for the bridge, cursed the sleepy Wang and sent him below. A moment later the yacht swung and held steadily, a little off shore. They were nowhere near the head of the gulf, but undoubtedly well past Chinchow and the end of the Great Wall, so that the mountains rising to the left were certainly Manchurian soil.

Stanley, yawning, appeared on the starboard ladder. Connor was calling to him, when he stiffened abruptly. From somewhere below lifted the sharp explosion of a pistol.

"Engine-room on the jump, Stanley!" exclaimed Connor. "That's vital. Whatever happens, keep control there. I'll see to things here."

Stanley disappeared. Connor jumped for the port ladder and slid down. As he struck the deck, Wang appeared before him, his long knife running blood.

"Quick, master!" broke out his panting cry. "The captain smashed his door and got out. He ran aft. There was a Japanese soldier with him, who shot one of our men. I got him—"

"A Japanese! Are you sure?"

Wang pointed down the passage. "There is his body."

Connor broke aft at a run. He nearly stumbled over the body of a Japanese officer in uniform. Impossible as it seemed, it was true. Something of the explanation flashed over him in this ghastly instant. Farson had broken out. Somewhere aboard there must have been Japanese in hiding—and Farson had gone aft! Another shot and another rang out.

Connor came to an abrupt halt as he cleared the superstructure. Before him lay the after-deck, and at the companion-way he saw two of his Manchus. Both had been shot down. One of them was weakly trying to throw up his weapon. Plunging across the deck at them were four little brown men in uniform, accompanied by Farson.

Without hesitation, Connor grimly threw up his pistol and pressed the trigger. Farson spun around and pitched sideways. The dying Manchu fired pointblank and one of the Japanese fell almost on top of him. The others separated, broke back for cover—but not before the amazed Connor recognized one of them as Colonel Honzai.

Two shots cracked out. Connor felt one of the bullets twitch at his hair.

"Wang! Wait here, bide your time, get down to the cabins to our Manchu friends."

"I can go through the ship from forward, Master."

"Do it, then. Bring him up to the bridge," snapped Connor.

He hurriedly retraced his steps. As he reached the cross passage into which the cabins of the officers opened, he came face to face with Galloway, who wildly waved a pistol.

"Ye fool, hands up!" yelled the chief. "The ship's ours—"

Connor shot him between the eyes.

A CABIN door smashed open, a pistol erupted almost in his face. His own weapon spurted flame until the hammer clicked on nothing. A Japanese face grinned at him in ghastly wise, and over the body tripped Hawkins, plunging forward, coughing as he died. No others. Connor caught up the unused pistol from the hand of Hawkins, dropped his own empty weapon, and dashed for the ladder.

He was halfway to the bridge again, when an outburst of yells and shots came from the forward deck. He glanced around, and a groan broke from him. The crew were loose, and knives were flashing in the level sunlight; two of his Manchus were in the midst, shooting. One of them went down, then the other. The Chinese scattered.

Only Jung Toy remained of his six men, unless he were also dead.

Connor came to the bridge. An oath broke from him, as he saw a signal fluttering up the halliards. Two Japanese stood there, behind the bridge, absorbed in their task. They faced about swiftly, flung up their weapons, but too late, Connor's bullets brought them down with relentless precision. Glancing about the horizon, Connor saw that the smoke to the northeast had become a long, low hull, evidently racing to meet them.

He started into the pilot-house, whistled down the tube. Stanley made response.

"All serene down here. Just bagged two Japanese. What's up?"

"Honzai's aboard with a bunch of men. Can you hang on there for five minutes?"

"You bet."

"Good. When I ring for half speed, drop everything and get up here on the jump."

"Attaboy! Shoot the works!"

Already Connor's hand had swung the steering gear. The yacht swerved a little, headed straight for the shore. Two miles away, or less. She was at full speed, water spurting from her sharp bows. Ten minutes at the outside, figured Connor.

He straightened up, wiping a blur from his eyes—blood. He was hurt, but had felt no pain where a bullet had gashed across his forehead. He winced as his fingers touched the place. Putting down the pistol, he got out his handkerchief twisted it about his head, and knotted it, to keep the blood from his eyes.

A spurt leaped in the water, dead ahead. Then the heavy bark of a gun. The destroyer, now coming in to overhaul them, loomed larger each instant. Connor looked at the rocky, hilly coast ahead, and his eyes were hard as flint. Two minutes, three minutes had gone. The scrape of feet sounded on the ladder, and he caught up his pistol.

IT WAS Wang who appeared. After him came the lean, dark Jung Toy, who turned and gave his hand to help his master; Connor saw blood running down from his brown fingers. Then appeared the last of the Manchus, and Connor gave him a surprised glance. The young man was very pale and had lost his spectacles. He was wearing a fur-trimmed robe of yellow brocaded silk, and this had changed his entire appearance. He had suddenly become an emperor, a Manchu, the son of heaven indeed. Stripping the Occidental garments from him, made him what he was.

"What has happened?" he asked, blinking around.

"Nothing," said Connor grimly, and motioned the others into the bridge-house.

Five minutes, six, had elapsed. The shore was closer now. Black ragged reefs stretched out into the water ahead. He leaped swiftly to the controls. The yacht's course changed slightly. She headed straight between two of the reefs, where showed black jutting rocks coming close up to the strip of beach.

Connor put out his hand to the engine-room telegraph and swung the lever to half speed.

A scream rang out overhead, a shell burst on the shore among the rocks; the sharper report of the gun floated after. The destroyer had plowed down close, within half a mile.

"Mr. Connor!" sounded a shrill voice from below. "Mr. Connor! May I come up?"

"Come on," responded Connor grimly.

Colonel Honzai appeared, ascending the port ladder, his hands empty. He was in uniform. As he caught sight of the last of the Manchu emperors, he saluted respectfully. Connor swung over the lever to "stop," trusting that someone below would heed the signal, and darted out to the bridge-rail, gripping it hard. With a rush, Stanley appeared, pistol in hand. Honzai began to speak, but a shrill and terrible yell of fright arose from the decks below. He swung around and saw the black rocks swooping for them.

"Hang on, everybody!" shouted Connor.

Stanley joined him, caught hold of him and of the rail. Colonel Honzai, aghast, joined both of them. There was one moment of utter stupefaction, as the yacht sped between the reefs. Her speed had slackened, her engines had ceased—someone had obeyed that final order. Another outburst of yells and cries from below.

Then a tremendous crash. A violent lurch, an awful sound of splintering, rending, smashing. The act of a madman had been accomplished.

A SECOND shock. The whole vessel shuddered and shook, crash followed crash as the masts splintered, the smokestack toppled over. With the bottom ripped out of her, the yacht staggered to rest. Her prow heaved up on the sand of the shore as she canted over sharply to starboard.

Connor dizzily came to his feet, shoved his pistol into the face of Honzai.

"Hands up! Cover him, Stanley!"

Stanley, clawing himself erect, obeyed the command. Connor turned into the bridge-house, caught the emperor by the shoulders, helped him up. Wang was already on his feet. Jung Toy rose more slowly, then sank back on his knees, and prostrated himself before the man in the yellow robe.

"Son of heaven!" he said in a faint voice. "Son of heaven—"

His head fell forward on his blood-black hands. His body relaxed, then tumbled suddenly sideways and fell, sprawling, into the scuppers. Connor caught the dazed Hsuan by the arm and led him outside, and pointed.

"Come!" he cried out, his voice ringing vibrantly. "We're ashore, do you understand? It's over. We'll get away before that destroyer can land men. We've won the game!"

"You had better surrender," said Colonel Honzai. "I have three men left—"

"And you're a prisoner." Connor flung an exultant laugh at him, and turned to Hsuan. "We'll clear the way, Your Majesty! The game's won! Follow us, set foot on Manchurian soil, your own soil, the land of your fathers! Stanley, clear the way, and I'll follow with him!"

"Attaboy!" boomed the wild, reckless voice of Stanley. "Hurray! We'll make the grade—"

"Stop!"

The last of the Manchus lifted his head. Suddenly his figure had come erect. A new light flashed in his eyes, a new firmness showed in his flaccid features. Even Connor, despite his agony of haste, was checked by this look, this manner, this voice. The blood of Nurhachu had come to life at last, for one vibrant moment.

"Colonel Honzai!" he exclaimed. "These two white men and their servant have done their best for me, have accomplished miracles. If I place myself in your hands, will you swear by the emperor whom you hold sacred that they shall not be harmed, but returned to Tientsin, free and unhindered?"

"I swear it!" The Nipponese drew himself up and saluted. "By the sacred imperial house—"

"No!"

THE CRY burst front Connor. He whirled, flung out his hand at the Manchu. His face was contorted, touched with blood from his wound. His voice was hoarse, agonized, terrible to hear.

"Listen! Look! There's plenty of time, plenty! They're just lowering boats—we'll break the way for you, get you ashore, take you safe inland! Don't give up, when men have died to get you here, when Jung Toy gave his heart's blood for you—don't give up! Play out the game, go down fighting if you must—"

"No," said the Manchu, and the word was firm and hard as a blow. His eyes met the strained gaze of Connor with implacable resolution.

"My friend, you do not understand. I resign you, I resign everything. I refuse to have more men die for me. I do not want war and death, in order that I may sit upon a throne. I want peace! When I agreed to your plan the other night, I was drunk with wine. Now I shall retire within myself and seek peace. Colonel Honzai, you are of the noblest blood in Japan. Your honor is inviolate. I bargain for these men, not for myself. I accept your word."

The officer bowed respectfully and drew in his breath with a hiss, after the custom of his people.

"My word is pledged," he said.

Connor looked at them, his face white as death. Then he heaved up his arm, flung his pistol out over the rail, and staggered. The strong arm of Stanley caught him.

So the last of the Tsing dynasty passed over the sea to Dairen, and whether to a throne or to some darker destiny, Connor did not know for a long while afterward. Nor, to tell the truth, did he care greatly, for his heart was bitter.

But Earl Stanley laughed his great laugh, and went booming on down the China coasts in search of what he might find awaiting him.

H . BEDFORD-JONES

BEDFORD-JONES IS a Canadian by birth, but not by profession, having removed to the United States at the age of one year. For over twenty years he has been more or less profitably engaged in writing and traveling. As he has seldom resided in one place longer than a year or so and is a person of retiring habits, he is somewhat a man of mystery; more than once he has suffered from unscrupulous gentlemen who impersonated him—one of whom murdered a wife and was subsequently shot by the police, luckily after losing his alias.

The real Bedford-Jones is an elderly man, whose gray hair and precise attire give him rather the appearance of a retired foreign diplomat. His hobby is stamp collecting, and his collection of Japan is said to be one of the finest in existence. At present writing he is en route to Morocco, and when this appears in print he will probably be somewhere on the Mojave Desert in company with Erle Stanley Gardner.

Questioned as to the main facts in his life, he declared there was only one main fact, but it was not for publication; that his life had been uneventful except for numerous financial losses, and that his only adventures lay in evading adventurers. In his younger years he was something of an athlete, but the encroachments of age preclude any active pursuits except that of motoring. He is usually to be found poring over his stamps, working at his typewriter, or laboring in his California rose garden, which is one of the sights of Cathedral Cañon, near Palm Springs.

Bedford-Jones has written stories laid in many corners of the earth, but among his most popular tales were the John Solomon stories which started many years ago in the *Argosy*.